Scattered throughout the stars they live—
these alien but intelligent beings. Some day
we will find them or they will find us. Maybe
these things will happen:

- Burt is just an ordinary guy going about
  his usual business. Then a runaway from
  outer space takes over his body, his mind,
  his girl

- The human race is expanding throughout
  the galaxy—and so is an alien race. Then
  these two growing empires meet

- Men finally pierce the mysterious cloud
  cover of Venus—and learn that even in
  our own solar system strange life forms
  exist

These and other tales will hold you spell-
bound, as Murray Leinster explores the weird
and wonderful possibilities of other life on
other worlds.

THE
ALIENS

Murray Leinster

A BERKLEY MEDALLION BOOK
published by
THE BERKLEY PUBLISHING CORPORATION

The Aliens

AT 04 HOURS 10 minutes, ship time, the *Niccola* was well inside the Theta Gisol solar system. She had previously secured excellent evidence that this was not the home of the Plumie civilization. There was no tuned radiation. There was no evidence of interplanetary travel—rockets would be more than obvious, and a magnetronic drive had a highly characteristic radiation-pattern—so the real purpose of the *Niccola's* voyage would not be accomplished here. She wouldn't find out where Plumies came from.

There might, though, be one or more of those singular, conical, hollow-topped cairns sheltering silicon-bronze plates, which constituted the evidence that Plumies existed. The *Niccola* went sunward toward the inner planets to see. Such cairns had been found on conspicuous landmarks on oxygen-type planets over a range of some twelve hundred light-years. By the vegetation about them, some were a century old. On the same evidence, others had been erected only months or weeks or even days before a human Space Survey ship arrived to discover them. And the situation was unpromising. It wasn't likely that the galaxy was big enough to hold two races of rational beings capable of space travel. Back on ancient Earth, a planet had been too small to hold two races with tools and fire. Historically, that problem was settled when *Homo sapiens* exterminated *Homo neanderthalis.* It appeared that the same situation had arisen in space. There were humans, and there were Plumies. Both had interstellar ships. To humans, the fact was alarming. The need for knowledge, and the danger that Plumies might know more first, and thereby be able to exterminate humanity, was appalling.

Therefore the *Niccola.* She drove on sunward. She had left one frozen outer planet far behind. She had crossed the orbits of three others. The last of these was a gas giant with innumerable moonlets revolving about it. It was now some thirty millions of miles back and twenty to one side. The sun, ahead, flared and flamed in emptiness against that expanse of tinted stars.

5

Jon Baird worked steadily in the *Niccola's* radar room. He was one of those who hoped that the Plumies would not prove to be the natural enemies of mankind. Now, it looked like this ship wouldn't find out in this solar system. There were plenty of other ships on the hunt. From here on, it looked like routine to the next unvisited family of planets. But meanwhile he worked. Opposite him, Diane Holt worked as steadily, her dark head bent intently over a radar graph in formation. The immediate job was the completion of a map of the meteor swarms following cometary orbits about this sun. They interlaced emptiness with hazards to navigation, and nobody would try to drive through a solar system without such a map.

Elsewhere in the ship, everything was normal. The engine room was a place of stillness and peace, save for the almost inaudible hum of the drive, running at half a million Gauss flux-density. The skipper did whatever skippers do when they are invisible to their subordinates. The weapons officer, Taine, thought appropriate thoughts. In the navigation room the second officer conscientiously glanced at each separate instrument at least once in each five minutes, and then carefully surveyed all the screens showing space outside the ship. The stewards disposed of the debris of the last meal, and began to get ready for the next. In the crew's quarters, those off duty read or worked at scrimshaw, or simply and contentedly loafed.

Diane handed over the transparent radar graph, to be fitted into the three-dimensional map in the making.

"There's a lump of stuff here," she said interestedly. "It could be the comet that once followed this orbit, now so old it's lost all its gases and isn't a comet any longer."

At this instant, which was 04 hours 25 minutes ship time, the alarm-bell rang. It clanged stridently over Baird's head, repeater-gongs sounded all through the ship, and there was a scurrying and a closing of doors. The alarm gong could mean only one thing. It made one's breath come faster or one's hair stand on end, according to temperament.

The skipper's face appeared on the direct-line screen from the navigation room.

"*Plumies?*" he demanded harshly. "*Mr. Baird! Plumies?*"

Baird's hands were already flipping switches and plugging the radar room apparatus into a new setup.

"There's a contact, sir," he said curtly. "No. There was a contact. It's broken now. Something detected us. We picked up a radar pulse. One."

6

The word "one" meant much. A radar system that could get adequate information from a single pulse was not, the work of amateurs. It was the product of a very highly developed technology. Setting all equipment to full-globular scanning, Baird felt a certain crawling sensation at the back of his neck. He'd been mapping within a narrow range above and below the line of this system's ecliptic. A lot could have happened outside the area he'd had under long-distance scanning.

But seconds passed. They seemed like years. The all-globe scanning covered every direction out from the *Niccola.* Nothing appeared which had not been reported before. The gas-giant planet far behind, and the only inner one on this side of the sun, would return their pulses only after minutes. Meanwhile the radars reported very faintfully, but they only repeated previous reports.

"No new object within half a million miles," said Baird, after a suitable interval. Presently he added: "Nothing new within three-quarter million miles." Then: "Nothing new within a million miles . . ."

The skipper said bitingly:

"Then you'd better check on objects that are not new!" He turned aside, and his voice came more faintly as he spoke into another microphone. *"Mr. Taine! Arm all rockets and have your tube crews stand by in combat readiness! Engine room! Prepare drive for emergency maneuvers! Damage-control parties, put on pressure suits and take combat posts with equipment!"* His voice rose again in volume. *"Mr. Baird! How about observed objects?"*

Diane murmured. Baird said briefly:

"Only one suspicious object, sir—and that shouldn't be suspicious. We are sending an information-beam at something we'd classed as a burned-out comet. Pulse going out now, sir."

Diane had the distant-information transmitter aimed at what she'd said might be a dead comet. Baird pressed the button. An extraordinary complex of information-seeking frequencies and forms sprang into being and leaped across emptiness. There were microwaves of strictly standard amplitude, for measurement-standards. There were frequencies of other values, which would be selectively absorbed by this material and that. There were laterally and circularly polarized beams. When they bounced back, they would bring a surprising amount of information.

They returned. They did bring back news. The thing that had registered as a larger lump in a meteorswarm was not

7

a meteor at all. It returned four different frequencies with a relative-intensity pattern which said that they'd been reflected by bronze—probably silicon bronze. The polarized beams came back depolarized, of course, but with phase-changes which said the reflector had a rounded, regular form. There was a smooth hull of silicon bronze out yonder. There was other data.

"It will be a Plumie ship, sir," said Baird very steadily. "At a guess, they picked up our mapping beam and shot a single pulse at us to find out who and what we were. For another guess, by now they've picked up and analyzed our information-beam and know what we've found out about them."

The skipper scowled.

"How many of them?" he demanded. *"Have we run into a fleet?"*

"I'll check, sir," said Baird. "We picked up no tuned radiation from outer space, sir, but it could be that they picked us up when we came out of overdrive and stopped all their transmissions until they had us in a trap."

"Find out how many there are!" barked the skipper. *"Make it quick! Report additional data instantly!"*

His screen clicked off. Diane, more than a little pale, worked swiftly to plug the radar-room equipment into a highly specialized pattern. The *Niccola* was very well equipped, radarwise. She's been a type G8 Survey ship, and on her last stay in port she'd been rebuilt especially to hunt for and make contact with Plumies. Since the discovery of their existence, that was the most urgent business of the Space Survey. It might well be the most important business of the human race—on which its survival or destruction would depend. Other remodeled ships had gone out before the *Niccola*, and others would follow until the problem was solved. Meanwhile the *Niccola's* twenty-four rocket tubes and stepped-up drive and computer-type radar system equipped her for Plumie-hunting as well as any human ship could be. Still, if she'd been lured deep into the home system of the Plumies, the prospects were not good.

The new setup began its operation, instantly the last contact closed. The three-dimensional map served as a matrix to control it. The information-beam projector swung and flung out its bundle of oscillations. It swung and flashed, and swung and flashed. It had to examine every relatively nearby object for a constitution of silicon bronze and a rounded shape. The nearest objects had to be examined first.

Speed was essential. But three-dimensional scanning takes time, even at some hundreds of pulses per minute.

Nevertheless, the information came in. No other silicon-bronze object within a quarter-million miles. Within half a million. A million. A million and a half. Two million . . . Baird called the navigation room.

"Looks like a single Plumie ship, sir," he reported. "At least there's one ship which is nearest by a very long way."

"*Hah!*" grunted the skipper. "*Then we'll pay him a visit. Keep an open line, Mr. Baird!*" His voice changed. "*Mr. Taine! Report here at once to plan tactics!*"

Baird shook his head, to himself. The *Niccola's* orders were to make contact without discovery, if such a thing were possible. The ideal would be a Plumie ship or the Plumie civilization itself, located and subject to complete and overwhelming envelopment by human ships—before the Plumies knew they'd been discovered. And this would be the human ideal because humans have always had to consider that a stranger might be hostile, until he'd proven otherwise.

Such a viewpoint would not be optimism, but caution. Yet caution was necessary. It was because the Survey brass felt the need to prepare for every unfavorable eventuality that Taine had been chosen as weapons officer of the *Niccola*. His choice had been deliberate, because he was a xenophobe. He had been a problem personality all his life. He had a seemingly congenital fear and hatred of strangers—which in mild cases is common enough, but Taine could not be cured without a complete breakdown of personality. He could not serve on a ship with a multiracial crew, because he was invincibly suspicious of and hostile to all but his own small breed. Yet he seemed ideal for weapons officer on the *Niccola*, provided he never commanded the ship. Because *if* the Plumies were hostile, a well-adjusted, normal man would never think as much like them as a Taine. He was capable of the kind of thinking Plumies might practice, if they were xenophobes themselves.

But to Baird, so extreme a precaution as a known psychopathic condition in an officer was less than wholly justified. It was by no means certain that the Plumies would instinctively be hostile. Suspicious, yes. Cautious, certainly. But the only fact known about the Plumie civilization came from the cairns and silicon-bronze inscribed tablets they'd left on oxygen-type worlds over a twelve-hundred-light-year range in space, and the only thing to be deduced about the Plumies themselves came from the decorative, formalized

9

symbols like feathery plumes which were found on all their bronze tablets. The name "Plumies" came from that symbol.

Now, though, Taine was called to the navigation room to confer on tactics. The *Niccola* swerved and drove toward the object Baird identified as a Plumie ship. This was at 05 hours 10 minutes ship time. The human ship had a definite velocity, sunward, of course. The Plumie ship had been concealed by the meteor swarm of a totally unknown comet. It was an excellent way to avoid observation. On the other hand, the *Niccola* had been mapping, which was bound to attract attention. Now each ship knew of the other's existence. Since the *Niccola* had been detected, she had to carry out orders and attempt a contact to gather information.

Baird verified that the *Niccola's* course was exact for interception at her full-drive speed. He said in a flat voice:

"I wonder how the Plumies will interpret this change of course? They know we're aware they're not a meteorite. But charging at them without even trying to communicate could look ominous. We could be stupid, or too arrogant to think of anything but a fight." He pressed the skipper's call and said evenly: "Sir, I request permission to attempt to communicate with the Plumie ship. We're ordered to try to make friends if we know we've been spotted."

Taine had evidently just reached the navigation room. His voice snapped from the speaker:

"*I advise against that, sir! No use letting them guess our level of technology!*"

Baird said coldly:

"They've a good idea already. We beamed them for data."

There was silence, with only the very faint humming sound which was natural in the ship in motion. It would be deadly to the nerves if there were absolute silence. The skipper grumbled:

"*Requests and advice! Dammit! Mr. Baird, you might wait for orders! But I was about to ask you to try to make contact through signals. Do so.*"

His speaker clicked off. Baird said:

"It's in our laps, Diane. And yet we have to follow orders. Send the first roll."

Diane had a tape threaded into a transmitter. It began to unroll through a pickup head. She put on headphones. The tapes began to transmit toward the Plumie. Back at base it had been reasoned that a pattern of clickings, plainly artificial and plainly stating facts known to both races, would be the most reasonable way to attempt to open contact. The tape sent a series of cardinal numbers—one to five. Then an addition table, from one plus one to five plus five. Then a multiplication table up to five times five. It was not startling intellectual information to be sent out in tiny clicks ranging up and down the radio spectrum. But it was orders.

Baird sat with compressed lips. Diane listened for a repetition of any of the transmitted signals, sent back by the Plumie. The speakers about the radar room murmured the orders given through all the ship. Radar had to be informed of all orders and activity, so it could check their results outside the ship. So Baird heard the orders for the engine room to be sealed up and the duty-force to get into pressure suits, in case the *Niccola* fought and was hulled. Damage-control parties reported themselves on post, in suits, with equipment ready. Then Taine's voice snapped: *"Rocket crews, arm even-numbered rockets with chemical explosive warheads. Leave odd-numbered rockets armed with atomics. Report back!"*

Diane strained her ears for possible re-transmission of the *Niccola's* signals, which would indicate the Plumie's willingness to try conversation. But she suddenly raised her hand and pointed to the radar-graph instrument. It repeated the positioning of dots which were stray meteoric matter in the space between worlds in this system. What had been a spot —the Plumie ship—was now a line of dots. Baird pressed the button.

"Radar reporting!" he said curtly. "The Plumie ship is heading for us. I'll have relative velocity in ten seconds."

He heard the skipper swear. Ten seconds later the Doppler measurement became possible. It said the Plumie plunged toward the *Niccola* at miles per second. In half a minute it was tens of miles per second. There was no re-transmission of signals. The Plumie ship had found itself discovered. Apparently it considered itself attacked. It flung itself into a headlong dash for the *Niccola*.

Time passed—interminable time. The sun flared and flamed and writhed in emptiness. The great gas-giant planet rolled through space in splendid state, its moonlets spinning gracefully about its bulk. The oxygen-atmosphere planet to sunward was visible only as a crescent, but the mottlings on its lighted part changed as it revolved—seas and islands and continents receiving the sunlight as it turned. Meteor swarms, so dense in appearance on a radar screen, yet so tenuous in

11

reality, floated in their appointed orbits with a seeming vast leisure.

The feel of slowness was actually the result of distance. Men have always acted upon things close by. Battles have always been fought within eye-range, anyhow. But it was actually 06 hours 35 minutes ship time before the two spacecraft sighted each other—more than two hours after they plunged toward a rendezvous.

The Plumie ship was a bright golden dot, at first. It decelerated swiftly. In minutes it was a rounded, end-on disk. Then it swerved lightly and presented an elliptical broadside to the *Niccola*. The *Niccola* was in full deceleration too, by then. The two ships came very nearly to a stop with relation to each other when they were hardly twenty miles apart—which meant great daring on both sides.

Baird heard the skipper grumbling:

"Damned cocky!" He roared suddenly: *"Mr. Baird! How've you made out in communicating with them?"*

"Not at all, sir," said Baird grimly. "They don't reply."

He knew from Diane's expression that there was no sound in the headphones except the frying noise all main-sequence stars give out, and the infrequent thumping noises that come from gas-giant planets' lower atmospheres, and the Jansky-radiation hiss which comes from everywhere.

The skipper swore. The Plumie ship lay broadside to, less than a score of miles away. It shone in the sunlight. It acted with extraordinary confidence. It was as if it dared the *Niccola* to open fire.

Taine's voice came out of a speaker, harsh and angry:

"Even-numbered tubes prepare to fire on command."

Nothing happened. The two ships floated sunward together, neither approaching nor retreating. But with every second, the need for action of some sort increased.

"Mr. Baird!" barked the skipper. *"This is ridiculous! There must be some way to communicate! We can't sit here glaring at each other forever! Raise them! Get some sort of acknowledgement!"*

"I'm trying," said Baird bitterly, "according to orders!"

But he disagreed with those orders. It was official theory that arithmetic values, repeated in proper order, would be the way to open conversation. The assumption was that any rational creature would grasp the idea that orderly signals were rational attempts to open communication.

But it had occurred to Baird that a Plumie might not see this point. Perception of order is not necessarily perception of information—in fact, quite the contrary. A message is a disturbance of order. A microphone does not transmit a message when it sends an unvarying tone. A message has to be unpredictable or it conveys no message. Orderly clicks, even if overheard, might seem to Plumies the result of methodically operating machinery. A race capable of interstellar flight was not likely to be interested or thrilled by exercises a human child goes through in kindergarten. They simply wouldn't seem meaningful at all.

But before he could ask permission to attempt to make talk in a more sophisticated fashion, voices exclaimed all over the ship. They came blurringly to the loud-speakers. *"Look at that!" "What's he do—" "Spinning like—"* From every place where there was a vision-plate on the *Niccola*, men watched the Plumie ship and babbled.

This was at 06 hours 50 minutes ship time.

The elliptical golden object darted into swift and eccentric motion. Lacking an object of known size for comparison, there was no scale. The golden ship might have been the size of an autumn leaf, and in fact its maneuvers suggested the heedless tumblings and scurrying of falling foliage. It fluttered in swift turns and somersaults and spinnings. There were weavings like the purposeful feints of boxers not yet come to battle. There were indescribably graceful swoops and loops and curving dashes like some preposterous dance in emptiness.

Taine's voice crashed out of a speaker:

"All even-numbered rockets," he barked. *"Fire!"*

The skipper roared a countermand, but too late. The crunching, grunting sound of rockets leaving their launching tubes came before his first syllable was complete. Then there was silence while the skipper gathered breath for a masterpiece of profanity. But Taine snapped:

"That dance was a sneak-up! The Plumie came four miles nearer while we watched!"

Baird jerked his eyes from watching the Plumie. He looked at the master radar. It was faintly blurred with the fading lines of past gyrations, but the golden ship was much nearer the *Niccola* than it had been.

"Radar reporting," said Baird sickishly. "Mr. Taine is correct. The Plumie ship did approach us while it danced."

Taine's voice snarled:

"Reload even numbers with chemical-explosive war heads. Then remove atomics from odd numbers and replace with chemicals. The range is too short for atomics."

Baird felt curiously divided in his own mind. He disliked

13

Taine very much. Taine was arrogant and suspicious and intolerant even on the *Niccola*. But Taine had been right twice, now. The Plumie ship had crept closer by pure trickery. And it was right to remove atomic war heads from the rockets. They had a pure-blast radius of ten miles. To destroy the Plumie ship within twice that would endanger the *Niccola*—and leave nothing of the Plumie to examine afterward.

The Plumie ship must have seen the rocket flares, but it continued to dance, coming nearer and ever nearer in seemingly heedless and purposeless plungings and spinnings in star-speckled space. But suddenly there were racing, rushing trails of swirling vapor. Half the *Niccola's* port broadside plunged toward the golden ship. The fraction of a second later, the starboard half-dozen chemical-explosive rockets swung furiously around the ship's hull and streaked after their brothers. They moved in utterly silent, straight-lined, ravening ferocity toward their target. Baird thought irrelevantly of the vapor trails of an atmosphere-liner in the planet's upper air.

The ruled-line straightness of the first six rockets' course abruptly broke. One of them veered crazily out of control. It shifted to an almost right-angled course. A second swung wildly to the left. A third and fourth and fifth—The sixth of the first line of rockets made a great, sweeping turn and came hurtling back toward the *Niccola*. It was like a nightmare. Lunatic, erratic lines of sunlit vapor eeled before the background of all the stars in creation.

Then the second half-dozen rockets broke ranks, as insanely and irremediably as the first.

Taine's voice screamed out of a speaker, hysterical with fury:

"Detonate! Detonate! They've taken over the rockets and are throwing 'em back at us! Detonate all rockets!"

The heavens seemed streaked and laced with lines of expanding smoke. But now one plunging line erupted at its tip. A swelling globe of smoke marked its end. Another blew up. And another—

The *Niccola's* rockets faithfully blew themselves to bits on command from the *Niccola's* own weapons control. There was nothing else to be done with them. They'd been taken over in flight. They'd been turned and headed back toward their source. They'd have blasted the *Niccola* to bits but for their premature explosions.

There was a peculiar, stunned hush all through the *Niccola*. The only sound that came out of any speaker in the

14

radar room was Taine's voice, high-pitched and raging, mouthing unspeakable hatred of the Plumies, whom no human being had yet seen.

Baird sat tense in the frustrated and desperate composure of the man who can only be of use while he is sitting still and keeping his head. The vision screen was now a blur of writhing mist, lighted by the sun and torn at by emptiness. There was luminosity where the ships had encountered each other. It was sunshine upon thin smoke. It was like the insanely enlarging head of a newborn comet, whose tail would be formed presently by light-pressure. The Plumie ship was almost invisible behind the unsubstantial stuff.

But Baird regarded his radar screens. Microwaves penetrated the mist of rapidly ionizing gases.

"Radar to navigation!" he said sharply. "The Plumie ship is still approaching, dancing as before!"

The skipper said with enormous calm:

"Any other Plumie ships, Mr. Baird?"

Diane interposed.

"No sign anywhere. I've been watching. This seems to be the only ship within radar range."

"We've time to settle with it, then," said the skipper. *"Mr. Taine, the Plumie ship is still approaching."*

Baird found himself hating the Plumies. It was not only that humankind was showing up rather badly, at the moment. It was that the Plumie ship had refused contact· and forced a fight. It was that if the *Niccola* were destroyed the Plumie would carry news of the existence of humanity and of the tactics which worked to defeat them. The Plumies could prepare an irresistible fleet. Humanity could be doomed.

But he overheard himself saying bitterly:

"I wish I'd known this was coming, Diane. I . . . wouldn't have resolved to be strictly official, only, until we got back to base."

Her eyes widened. She looked startled. Then she softened.

"If . . . you mean that . . . I wish so too."

"It looks like they've got us," he admitted unhappily. "If they can take our rockets away from us—" Then his voice stopped. He said, "Hold everything!" and pressed the navigation-room button. He snapped: "Radar to navigation. It appears to take the Plumies several seconds to take over a rocket. They have to aim something—a pressor or tractor beam, most likely—and pick off each rocket separately. Nearly forty seconds was consumed in taking over all twelve of our rockets. At shorter range, with less time available, a rocket might get through!"

The skipper swore briefly. Then:

"Mr. Taine! When the Plumies are near enough, our rockets may strike before they can be taken over! You follow?"

Baird heard Taine's shrill-voiced acknowledgment—in the form of practically chattered orders to his rocket-tube crews. Baird listened, checking the orders against what the situation was as the radars saw it. Taine's voice was almost unhuman; so filled with frantic rage that it cracked as he spoke. But the problem at hand was the fulfillment of all his psychopathic urges. He commanded the starboard-side rocket-battery to await special orders. Meanwhile the port-side battery would fire two rockets on widely divergent courses, curving to join at the Plumie ship. They'd be seized. They were to be detonated and another port-side rocket fired instantly, followed by a second hidden in the rocket-trail the first would leave behind. Then the starboard side—

"I'm afraid Taine's our only chance," said Baird reluctantly. "If he wins, we'll have time to . . . talk as people do who like each other. If it doesn't work—"

Diane said quietly:

"Anyhow . . . I'm glad you . . . wanted me to know. I . . . wanted you to know, too."

She smiled at him, yearningly.

There was the *crump-crump* of two rockets going out together. Then the radar told what happened. The Plumie ship was no more than six miles away, dancing somehow deftly in the light of a yellow sun, with all the cosmos spread out as shining pin points of colored light behind it. The radar reported the dash and the death of the two rockets, after their struggle with invisible things that gripped them. They died when they headed reluctantly back to the *Niccola*—and detonated two miles from their parent ship. The skipper's voice came:

"Mr. Taine! After your next salvo I shall head for the Plumie at full drive, to cut down the distance and the time they have to work in. Be ready!"

The rocket tubes went *crump-crump* again, with a fifth of a second interval. The radar showed two tiny specks speeding through space toward the weaving, shifting speck which was the Plumie.

Outside, in emptiness, there was a filmy haze. It was the rocket-fumes and explosive gases spreading with incredible speed. It was thin as gossamer. The Plumie ship undoubtedly

16

spotted the rockets, but it did not try to turn them. It somehow seized them and deflected them, and darted past them toward the *Niccola.*

"They see the trick," said Diane, dry-throated. "If they can get in close enough, they can turn it against us!"

There were noises inside the *Niccola,* now. Taine fairly howled an order. There were yells of defiance and excitement. There were more of those inadequate noises as rockets went out—every tube on the starboard side emptied itself in a series of savage grunts—and the *Niccola's* magnetronic drive roared at full flux density.

The two ships were less than a mile apart when the *Niccola* let go her full double broadside of missiles. And then it seemed that the Plumie ship was doomed. There were simply too many rockets to be seized and handled before at least one struck. But there was a new condition. The Plumie ship weaved and dodged its way through them. The new condition was that the rockets were just beginning their run. They had not achieved the terrific velocity they would accumulate in ten miles of no-gravity. They were new-launched; logy; clumsy: not the streaking, flashing death-and-destruction they would become with thirty more seconds of acceleration.

So the Plumie ship dodged them with a skill and daring past belief. With an incredible agility it got inside them, nearer to the *Niccola* than they. And then it hurled itself at the human ship as if bent upon a suicidal crash which would destroy both ships together. But Baird, in the radar room, and the skipper in navigation, knew that it would plunge brilliantly past at the last instant—

And then they knew that it would not. Because, very suddenly and very abruptly, there was something the matter with the Plumie ship. The life went out of it. It ceased to accelerate or decelerate. It ceased to steer. It began to turn slowly on an axis somewhere amidships. Its nose swung to one side, with no change in the direction of its motion. It floated onward. It was broadside to its line of travel. It continued to turn. It hurtled stern-first toward the *Niccola.* It did not swerve. It did not dance. It was a lifeless hulk: a derelict in space.

And it would hit the *Niccola* amidships with no possible result but destruction for both vessels.

The *Niccola's* skipper bellowed orders, as if shouting would somehow give them more effect. The magnetronic drive roared. He'd demanded a miracle of it, and he almost got one. The drive strained its thrust-members. It hopelessly over-

17

loaded its coils. The *Niccola's* cobalt-steel hull became more than saturated with the drive-field, and it leaped madly upon an evasion course—

And it very nearly got away. It was swinging clear when the Plumie ship drifted within fathoms. It was turning aside when the Plumie ship was within yards. And it was almost safe when the golden hull of the Plumie—shadowed now by the *Niccola* itself—barely scraped a side-keel.

There was a touch, seemingly deliberate and gentle. But the *Niccola* shuddered horribly. Then the vision screens flared from such a light as might herald the crack of doom. There was a brightness greater than the brilliance of the sun. And then there was a wrenching, heaving shock. Then there was blackness. Baird was flung across the radar room, and Diane cried out, and he careened against a wall and heard glass shatter. He called:

"Diane!"

He clutched crazily at anything, and called her name again. The *Niccola's* internal gravity was cut off, and his head spun, and he heard collision-doors closing everywhere, but before they closed completely he heard the rasping sound of giant arcs leaping in the engine room. Then there was silence.

"Diane!" cried Baird fiercely. "Diane!"

"I'm . . . here," she panted. "I'm dizzy, but I . . . think I'm all right—"

The battery-powered emergency light came on. It was faint, but he saw her clinging to a bank of instruments where she'd been thrown by the collision. He moved to go to her, and found himself floating in midair. But he drifted to a side wall and worked his way to her.

She clung to him, shivering.

"I . . . think," she said unsteadily, "that we're going to die. Aren't we?"

"We'll see," he told her. "Hold on to me."

Guided by the emergency light, he scrambled to the bank of communicator-buttons. What had been the floor was now a side wall. He climbed it and thumbed the navigation-room switch.

"Radar room reporting," he said curtly. "Power out, gravity off, no reports from outside from power failure. No great physical damage."

He began to hear other voices. There had never been an actual space-collision in the memory of man, but reports came crisply, and the cut-in speakers in the radar room repeated them. Ship-gravity was out all over the ship. Emergency lights were functioning, and those were all the lights there were. There was a slight, unexplained gravity-drift toward what had been the ship's port side. But damage-control reported no loss of pressure in the *Niccola's* inner hull, though four areas between inner and outer hulls had lost air pressure to space.

"*Mr. Baird*," rasped the skipper. "*We're blind! Forget everything else and give us eyes to see with!*"

"We'll try battery power to the vision plates," Baird told Diane. "No full resolution, but better than nothing—"

They worked together, feverishly. They were dizzy. Something close to nausea came upon them from pure giddiness. What had been the floor was now a wall, and they had to climb to each the instruments that had been on a wall and now were on the ceiling. But their weight was ounces only. Baird said abruptly:

"I know what's the matter! We're spinning! The whole ship's spinning! That's why we're giddy and why we have even a trace of weight. Centrifugal force! Ready for the current?"

There was a tiny click, and the battery light dimmed. But a vision screen lighted faintly. The stars it showed were moving specks of light. The sun passed deliberately across the screen. Baird switched to other outside scanners. There was power for only one screen at a time. But he saw the starkly impossible. He pressed the navigation-room button.

"Radar room reporting," he said urgently. "The Plumie ship is fast to us, in contact with our hull! Both ships are spinning together!" He was trying yet other scanners as he spoke, and now he said: "Got it! There are no lines connecting us to the Plumie, but it looks . . . yes! That flash when the ships came together was a flashover of high potential. We're welded to them along twenty feet of our hull!"

The skipper:

"*Damnation! Any sign of intention to board us?*"

"Not yet, sir—"

Taine burst in, his voice high-pitched and thick with hatred:

"*Damage-control parties attention! Arm yourselves and assemble at starboard air lock! Rocket crews get into suits and prepare to board this Plumie—*"

"*Countermand!*" bellowed the skipper from the speaker beside Baird's ear. "*Those orders are canceled! Dammit, if we were successfully boarded we'd blow ourselves to bits! Those are our orders! D'you think the Plumies will let their ship be taken? And wouldn't we blow up with them? Mr. Taine, you will take no offensive action without specific orders! Defen-*"

19

sive action is another matter. Mr. Baird! I consider this welding business pure accident. No one would be mad enough to plan it. You watch the Plumies and keep me informed!"

His voice ceased. And Baird had again the frustrating duty of remaining still and keeping his head while other men engaged in physical activity. He helped Diane to a chair—which was fastened to the floor-which-was-now-a-wall—and she wedged herself fast and began a review of what each of the outside scanners reported. Baird called for more batteries. Power for the radar and visions was more important than anything else, just then. If there were more Plumie ships . . .

Electricians half-floated, half-dragged extra batteries to the radar room. Baird hooked them in. The universe outside the ship again appeared filled with brilliantly colored dots of light which were stars. More satisfying, the globe-scanners again reported no new objects anywhere. Nothing new within a quarter million miles. A half-million. Later Baird reported:

"Radars report no strange objects within a million miles of the *Niccola*, sir."

"Except the ship we're welded to. But you are doing very well. However, microphones say there is movement inside the Plumie."

Diane beckoned for Baird's attention to a screen, which Baird had examined before. Now he stiffened and motioned for her to report.

"We've a scanner, sir," said Diane, "which faces what looks like a port in the Plumie ship. There's a figure at the port. I can't make out details, but it is making motions, facing us."

"Give me the picture!" snapped the skipper.

Diane obeyed. It was the merest flip of a switch. Then her eyes went back to the spherical-sweep scanners which reported the bearing and distance of every solid object within their range. She set up two instruments which would measure the angle, bearing, and distance of the two planets now on this side of the sun—the gas-giant and the oxygen-world to sunward. Their orbital speeds and distances were known. The position, course, and speed of the *Niccola* could be computed from any two observations on them.

Diane had returned to the utterly necessary routine of the radar room which was the nerve-center of the ship, gathering all information needed for navigation in space. The fact that there had been a collision, that the *Niccola's* engines were melted to unlovely scrap, that the Plumie ship was now welded irremovably to a sidekeel, and that a Plumie was signaling to humans while both ships went spinning through

20

space toward an unknown destination—these things did not affect the obligations of the radar room.

Baird got other images of the Plumie ship into sharp focus. So near, the scanners required adjustment for precision.

"Take a look at this!" he said wryly.

She looked. The view was of the Plumie as welded fast to the *Niccola*. The welding was itself an extraordinary result of the Plumie's battle-tactics. Tractor and pressor beams were known to men, of course, but human beings used them only under very special conditions. Their operation involved the building-up of terrific static charges. Unless a tractor-beam generator could be grounded to the object it was to pull, it tended to emit lightning-bolts at unpredictable intervals and in entirely random directions. So men didn't use them. Obviously, the Plumies did.

They'd handled the *Niccola's* rockets with beams which charged the golden ship to billions of volts. And when the silicon-bronze Plumie ship touched the cobalt-steel *Niccola*—why—that charge had to be shared. It must have been the most spectacular of all artificial electric flames. Part of the *Niccola's* hull was vaporized, and undoubtedly part of the Plumie. But the unvaporized surfaces were molten and in contact—and they stuck.

For a good twenty feet the two ships were united by the most perfect of vacuum-welds. The wholly dissimilar hulls formed a space-catamaran, with a sort of valley between their bulks. Spinning deliberately, as the united ships did, sometimes the sun shone brightly into that valley, and sometimes it was filled with the blackness of the pit.

While Diane looked, a round door revolved in the side of the Plumie ship. As Diane caught her breath, Baird reported crisply. At his first word Taine burst into raging commands for men to follow him through the *Niccola's* air lock and fight a boarding party of Plumies in empty space. The skipper very savagely ordered him to be quiet.

"Only one figure has come out," reported Baird. The skipper watched on a vision plate, but Baird reported so all the *Niccola's* company would know. "It's small—less than five feet . . . I'll see better in a moment." Sunlight smote down into the valley between the ships. "It's wearing a pressure suit. It seems to be the same material as the ship. It walks on two legs, as we do . . . It has two arms, or something very similar . . . The helmet of the suit is very high . . . It looks like the armor knights used to fight in . . . It's making its way to our air lock . . . It does not use magnetic-soled shoes.

21

It's holding onto lines threaded along the other ship's hull . . ."

The skipper said curtly:

"Mr. Baird! I hadn't noticed the absence of magnetic shoes. You seem to have an eye for important items. Report to the air lock in person. Leave Lieutenant Holt to keep an eye on outside objects. Quickly, Mr. Baird!"

Baird laid his hand on Diane's shoulder. She smiled at him. "I'll watch!" she promised.

He went out of the radar room, walking on what had been a side wall. The giddiness and dizziness of continued rotation was growing less, now. He was getting used to it. But the *Niccola* seemed strange indeed, with the standard up and down and Earth-gravity replaced by a vertical which was all askew and a weight of ounces instead of a hundred and seventh pounds.

He reached the air lock just as the skipper arrived. There were others there—armed and in pressure suits. The skipper glared about him.

"I am in command here," he said very grimly indeed. "Mr. Taine has a special function, but I am in command! We and the creatures on the Plumie ship are in a very serious fix. One of them apparently means to come on board. There will be no hostility, no sneering, no threatening gestures! This is a parley! You will be careful. But you will not be trigger-happy!"

He glared around again, just as a metallic rapping came upon the *Niccola's* air-lock door. The skipper nodded:

"Let him in the lock, Mr. Baird."

Baird obeyed. The humming of the unlocking-system sounded. There were clankings. The outer air lock closed. There was a faint whistling as air went in. The skipper nodded again.

Baird opened the inner door. It was 08 hours 10 minutes ship time.

The Plumie stepped confidently out into the topsy-turvy corridors of the *Niccola*. He was about the size of a ten-year-old human boy, and features which were definitely not grotesque showed through the clear plastic of his helmet. His pressure suit was, engineering-wise, a very clean job. His whole appearance was prepossessing. When he spoke, very clear and quite high sounds—soprano sounds—came from a small speaker-unit at his shoulder.

"For us to talk," said the skipper heavily, "is pure nonsense. But I take it you've something to say."

The Plumie gazed about with an air of lively curiosity. Then he drew out a flat pad with a white surface and sketched swiftly. He offered it to the *Niccola's* skipper.

"We want this on record," he growled, staring about.

Diane's voice said capably from a speaker somewhere nearby:

"Sir, there's a scanner for inspection of objects brought aboard. Hold the plate flat and I'll have a photograph—right!"

The skipper said curtly to the Plumie:

"You've drawn our two ships linked as they are. What have you to say about it?"

He handed back the plate. The Plumie pressed a stud and it was blank again. He sketched and offered it once more.

"Hm-m-m," said the skipper. "You can't use your drive while we're glued together, eh? Well?"

The Plumie reached up and added lines to the drawing.

"So!" rumbled the skipper, inspecting the additions. "You say it's up to us to use our drive for both ships." He growled approvingly: "You consider there's a truce. You must, because we're both in the same fix, and not a nice one, either. True enough! We can't fight each other without committing suicide, now. But we haven't any drive left! We're a derelict! How am I going to say that—if I decide to?"

Baird could see the lines on the plate, from the angle at which the skipper held it. He said:

"Sir, we've been mapping, up in the radar room. Those last lines are map-co-ordinates—a separate sketch, sir. I think he's saying that the two ships, together, are on a falling course toward the sun. That we have to do something or both vessels will fall into it. We should be able to check this, sir."

"Hah!" growled the skipper. "That's all we need! Absolutely all we need! To come here, get into a crazy fight, have our drive melt to scrap, get crazily welded to a Plumie ship, and then for both of us to fry together! We don't need anything more than that!"

Diane's voice came on the speaker:

"Sir, the last radar fixes on the planets in range give us a course directly toward the sun. I'll repeat the observations."

The skipper growled. Taine thrust himself forward. He snarled:

"Why doesn't this Plumie take off its helmet? It lands on oxygen planets! Does it think it's too good to breathe our air?"

Baird caught the Plumie's eye. He made a gesture suggesting the removal of the space helmet. The Plumie gestured, in return, to a tiny vent in the suit. He opened something and

23

gas whistled out. He cut it off. The question of why he did not open or remove his helmet was answered. The atmosphere he breathed would not do men any good, nor would theirs do him any good, either. Taine said suspiciously:

"How do we know he's breathing the stuff he let out then? This creature isn't human! It's got no right to attack humans! Now it's trying to trick us!" His voice changed to a snarl. "We'd better wring its neck! Teach its kind a lesson—"

The skipper roared at him.

"Be quiet! Our ship is a wreck! We have to consider the facts! We and these Plumies are in a fix together, and we have to get out of it before we start to teach anybody anything!" He glared at Taine. Then he said heavily: "Mr. Baird, you seem to notice things. Take this Plumie over the ship. Show him our drive melted down, so he'll realize we can't possibly tow his ship into an orbit. He knows that we're armed, and that we can't handle our war heads at this range! So we can't fool each other. We might as well be frank. But you will take full note of his reactions, Mr. Baird!"

Baird advanced, and the skipper made a gesture. The Plumie regarded Baird with interested eyes. And Baird led the way for a tour of the *Niccola*. It was confusing even to him, with right hand converted to up and left hand to down, and sidewise now almost vertical. On the way the Plumie made more clear, flutelike sounds, and more gestures. Baird answered.

"Our gravity pull was that way," he explained, "and things fell so fast."

He grasped a handrail and demonstrated the speed with which things fell in normal ship-gravity. He used a pocket communicator for the falling weight. It was singularly easy to say some things, even highly technical ones, because they'd be what the Plumie would want to know. But quite commonplace things would be very difficult to convey.

Diane's voice came out of the communicator.

"*There are no novelties outside,*" she said quietly. "*It looks like this is the only Plumie ship anywhere around. It could have been exploring, like us. Maybe it was looking for the people who put up Space-Survey markers.*"

"Maybe," agreed Baird, using the communicator. "Is that stuff about falling into the sun correct?"

"*It seems so,*" said Diane composedly. "*I'm checking again. So far, the best course I can get means we graze the sun's photosphere in fourteen days six hours, allowing for acceleration by the sun's gravity.*"

"And you and I," said Baird wryly, "have been acting as professional associates only, when—"

"Don't say it!" said Diane shakily. "It's terrible!"

He put the communicator back in his pocket. The Plumie had watched him. He had a peculiarly gallant air, this small figure in golden space armor with its high-crested helmet.

They reached the engine room. And there was the giant drive shaft of the Niccola, once wrapped with yard-thick coils which could induce an incredible density of magnetic flux in the metal. Even the return magnetic field, through the ship's cobalt-steel hull, was many times higher than saturation. Now the coils were sagging: mostly melted. There were places where re-solidified metal smoked noisomely against non-metallic floor or wall-covering. Engineers labored doggedly in the trivial gravity to clean up the mess.

"It's past repair," said Baird, to the ship's first engineer.

"It's junk," said that individual dourly. "Give us six months and a place to set up a wire-drawing mill and an insulator synthesizer, and we could rebuild it. But nothing less will be any good."

The Plumie stared at the drive. He examined the shaft from every angle. He inspected the melted, and partly-melted, and merely burned-out sections of the drive coils. He was plainly unable to understand in any fashion the principle of the magnetronic drive. Baird was tempted to try to explain, because there was surely no secret about a ship drive, but he could imagine no diagrams or gestures which would convey the theory of what happened in cobalt-steel when it was magnetized beyond one hundred thousand Gauss' flux-density. And without that theory one simply couldn't explain a magnetronic drive.

They left the engine room. They visited the rocket batteries. The generator room was burned out, like the drive, by the inconceivable lightning bolt which had passed between the ships on contact. The Plumie was again puzzled. Baird made it clear that the generator-room supplied electric current for the ship's normal lighting-system and services. The Plumie could grasp that idea. They examined the crew's quarters, and the mess room, and the Plumie walked confidently among the members of the human crew, who a little while since had tried so painstakingly to destroy his vessel. He made a good impression.

"These little guys," said a crewman to Baird, admiringly, "they got something. They can handle a ship! I bet they could almost make that ship of theirs play checkers!"

"Close to it," agreed Baird. He realized something. He

25

pulled the communicator from his pocket. "Diane! Contact the skipper. He wanted observations. Here's one. This Plumie acts like soldiers used to act in ancient days—when they wore armor. And we have the same reaction! They will fight like the devil, but during a truce they'll be friendly, admiring each other as scrappers, but ready to fight as hard as ever when the truce is over. We have the same reaction! Tell the skipper I've an idea that it's a part of their civilization—maybe it's a necessary part of any civilization! Tell him I guess that there may be necessarily parallel evolution of attitudes, among rational races, as there are parallel evolutions of eyes and legs and wings and fins among all animals everywhere! If I'm right, somebody from this ship will be invited to tour the Plumie! It's only a guess, but tell him!"

"*Immediately,*" said Diane.

The Plumie followed gallantly as Baird made a steep climb up what once was the floor of a corridor. Then Taine stepped out before them. His eyes burned.

"Giving him a clear picture, eh?" he rasped. "Letting him spy out everything?"

Baird pressed the communicator call for the radar room and said coldly:

"I'm obeying orders. Look, Taine! You were picked for your job because you were a xenophobe. It helps in your proper functioning. But this Plumie is here under a flag of truce—"

"Flag of truce!" snarled Taine. "It's vermin! It's not human! I'll—"

"If you move one inch nearer him," said Baird gently, "just one inch—"

The skipper's voice bellowed through the general call speakers all over the ship:

"*Mr. Taine! You will go to your quarters, under arrest! Mr. Baird, burn him down if he hesitates!*"

Then there was a rushing, and scrambling figures appeared and were all about. They were members of the *Niccola's* crew, sent by the skipper. They regarded the Plumie with detachment, but Taine with a wary expectancy. Taine turned purple with fury. He shouted. He raged. He called Baird and the others Plumie-lovers and vermin-worshipers. He shouted foulnesses at them. But he did not attack.

When, still shouting, he went away, Baird said apologetically to the Plumie:

"He's a xenophobe. He has a pathological hatred of strangers—even of strangeness. We have him on board because—"

Then he stopped. The Plumie wouldn't understand, of

26

course. But his eyes took on a curious look. It was almost as if, looking at Baird, they twinkled.

Baird took him back to the skipper.

"He's got the picture, sir," he reported.

The Plumie pulled out his sketch plate. He drew on it. He offered it. The skipper said heavily:

"You guessed right, Mr. Baird. He suggests that someone from this ship go on board the Plumie vessel. He's drawn two pressure-suited figures going in their air lock. One's larger than the other. Will you go?"

"Naturally!" said Baird. Then he added thoughtfully: "But I'd better carry a portable scanner, sir. It should work perfectly well through a bronze hull, sir."

The skipper nodded and began to sketch a diagram which would amount to an acceptance of the Plumie's invitation.

This was at 07 hours 40 minutes ship time. Outside the sedately rotating metal hulls—the one a polished blue-silver and the other a glittering golden bronze—the cosmos continued to be as always. The haze from explosive fumes and rocket-fuel was, perhaps, a little thinner. The brighter stars shone through it. The gas-giant planet outward from the sun was a perceptible disk instead of a diffuse glow. The oxygen-planet to sunward showed again as a lighted crescent.

Presently Baird, in a human spacesuit, accompanied the Plumie into the *Niccola's* air lock and out to emptiness. His magnetic-soled shoes clung to the *Niccola's* cobalt-steel skin. Fastened to his shoulder there was a tiny scanner and microphone, which would relay everything he saw and heard back to the radar room and to Diane.

She watched tensely as he went inside the Plumie ship. Other screens relayed the image and his voice to other places on the *Niccola*.

He was gone a long time. From the beginning, of course, there were surprises. When the Plumie escort removed his helmet, on his own ship, the reason for the helmet's high crest was apparent. He had a high crest of what looked remarkably like feathers—and it was not artificial. It grew there. The reason for conventionalized plumes on bronze survey plates was clear. It was exactly like the reason for human features or figures as decorative additions to the inscriptions on Space Survey marker plates. Even the Plumie's hands had odd crestlets which stood out when he bent his fingers. The other Plumies were no less graceful and no less colorful. They had equally clear soprano voices. They were equally miniature and so devoid of apparent menace.

But there were also technical surprises. Baird was taken

27

immediately to the Plumie ship's engine room, and Diane heard the sharp intake of breath with which he appeared to recognize its working principle. There were Plumie engineers working feverishly at it, attempting to discover something to repair. But they found nothing. The Plumie drive simply would not work.

They took Baird through the ship's entire fabric. And their purpose, when it became clear, was startling. The Plumie ship had no rocket tubes. It had no beam-projectors except small-sized objects which were—which must be—their projectors of tractor and pressor beams. They were elaborately grounded to the ship's substance. But they were not originally designed for ultra-heavy service. They hadn't and couldn't have the enormous capacity Baird had expected. He was astounded.

When he returned to the *Niccola,* he went instantly to the radar room to make sure that pictures taken through his scanner had turned out well. And there was Diane.

But the skipper's voice boomed at him from the wall.

"Mr. Baird! What have you to add to the information you sent back?"

"Three items, sir," said Baird. He drew a deep breath. "For the first, sir, the Plumie ship is unarmed. They've tractor and pressor beams for handling material. They probably use them to build their cairns. But they weren't meant for weapons. The Plumies, sir, hadn't a thing to fight with when they drove for us after we detected them."

The skipper blinked hard.

"Are you sure of that, Mr. Baird?"

"Yes, sir," said Baird uncomfortably. "The Plumie ship is an exploring ship—a survey ship, sir. You saw their mapping equipment. But when they spotted us, and we spotted them— they bluffed! When we fired rockets at them, they turned them back with tractor and pressor beams. They drove for us, sir, to try to destroy us with our own bombs, because they didn't have any of their own."

The skipper's mouth opened and closed.

"Another item, sir," said Baird more uncomfortably still. "They don't use iron or steel. Every metal object I saw was either a bronze or a light metal. I suspect some of their equipment's made of potassium, and I'm fairly sure they use sodium in the place of aluminum. Their atmosphere's quite different from ours—obviously! They'd use bronze for their ship's hull because they can venture into an oxygen atmosphere in a

28

bronze ship. A sodium-hulled ship would be lighter, but it would burn in oxygen. Where there was moisture—"

The skipper blinked.

"But they couldn't drive in a nonmagnetic hull!" he protested. *"A ship has to be magnetic to drive!"*

"Sir," said Baird, his voice still shaken, "they don't use a magnetronic drive. I once saw a picture of the drive they use, in a stereo on the history of space travel. The principle's very old. We've practically forgotten it. It's a Dirac pusher-drive, sir. Among us humans, it came right after rockets. The planets of Sol were first reached by ships using Dirac pushers. But—" He paused. "They won't operate in a magnetic field above seventy Gauss, sir. It's a static-charge reaction, sir, and in a magnetic field it simply stops working."

The skipper regarded Baird unwinkingly for a long time.

"I think you are telling me," he said at long last, *"that the Plumies' drive would work if they were cut free of the Niccola."*

"Yes, sir," said Baird. "Their engineers were opening up the drive-elements and checking them, and then closing them up again. They couldn't seem to find anything wrong. I don't think they know what the trouble is. It's the *Niccola's* magnetic field. I think it was our field that caused the collision by stopping their drive and killing all their controls when they came close enough."

"Did you tell them?" demanded the skipper.

"There was no easy way to tell them by diagrams, sir."

Taine's voice cut in. It was feverish. It was strident. It was triumphant.

"Sir! The Niccola *is effectively a wreck and unrepairable. But the Plumie ship is operable if cut loose. As weapons officer, I intend to take the Plumie ship, let out its air, fill its tanks with our air, start up its drive, and turn it over to you for navigation back to base!"*

Baird raged. But he said coldly:

"We're a long way from home, Mr. Taine, and the Dirac pusher drive is slow. If we headed back to base in the Plumie ship with its Dirac pusher, we'd all be dead of old age before we'd gone halfway."

"But unless we take it," raged Taine, *"we hit this sun in fourteen days! We don't have to die now! We can land on the oxygen planet up ahead! We've only to kill these vermin and take their ship, and we'll live!"*

Diane's voice said dispassionately:

"Report. A Plumie in a pressure suit just came out of their air lock. It's carrying a parcel toward our air lock."

29

Taine snarled instantly:

"They'll sneak something in the Niccola *to blast it, and then cut free and go away!"*

The skipper said very grimly:

"Mr. Taine, credit me with minimum brains! There is no way the Plumies can take this ship without an atomic bomb exploding to destroy both ships. You should know it!" Then he snapped: *"Air lock area, listen for a knock, and let in the Plumie or the parcel he leaves."*

There was silence. Baird said very quietly:

"I doubt they think it possible to cut the ships apart. A torch is no good on thick silicon bronze. It conducts heat too well! And they don't use steel. They probably haven't a cutting-torch at all."

From the radar room he watched the Plumie place an object in the air lock and withdraw. He watched from a scanner inside the ship as someone brought in what the Plumie had left. An electronics man bustled forward. He looked it over quickly. It was complex, but his examination suddenly seemed satisfying to him. But a grayish vapor developed and he sniffed and wrinkled his nose. He picked up a communicator.

"Sir, they've sent us a power-generator. Some of its parts are going bad in our atmosphere, sir, but this looks to me like a hell of a good idea for a generator! I never saw anything like it, but it's good! You can set it for any voltage and it'll turn out plenty juice!"

"Put it in helium," snapped the skipper. *"It won't break down in that! Then see how it serves!"*

In the radar room, Baird drew a deep breath. He went carefully to each of the screens and every radar. Diane saw what he was about, and checked with him. They met at the middle of the radar room.

"Everything's checked out," said Baird gravely. "There's nothing else around. There's nothing we can be called on to do before something happens. So . . . we can . . . act like people."

Diane smiled very faintly.

"Not like people. Just like us." She said wistfully: "Don't you want to tell me something? Something you intended to tell me only after we got back to base?"

He did. He told it to her. And there was also something she had not intended to tell him at all—unless he told her first. She said it now. They felt that such sayings were of the greatest possible importance. They clung together, saying them again. And it seemed wholly monstrous that two people

30

who cared so desperately had wasted so much time acting like professional associates—explorer-ship officers—when things like this were to be said . . .

As they talked incoherently, or were even more eloquently silent, the ship's ordinary lights came on. Thᶜ battery-lamp went on.

"We've got to switch back to ship's circuit," said Baird reluctantly. They separated, and restored the operating circuits to normal. "We've got fourteen days," he added, "and so much time to be on duty, and we've a lost lifetime to live in fourteen days! Diane—"

She flushed vividly. So Baird said very politely into the microphone to the navigation room:

"Sir, Lieutenant Hold and myself would like to speak directly to you in the navigation room. May we?"

"Why not?" growled the skipper. *"You've noticed that the Plumie generator is giving the whole ship lights and services?"*

"Yes, sir," said Baird. "We'll be there right away."

They heard the skipper's grunt as they hurried through the door. A moment later the ship's normal gravity returned—also through the Plumie generator. Up was up again, and down was down, and the corridors and cabins of the *Niccola* were brightly illuminated. Had the ship been other than an engineless wreck, falling through a hundred and fifty million miles of emptiness into the flaming photosphere of a sun, everything would have seemed quite normal, including the errand Baird and Diane were upon, and the fact that they held hands self-consciously as they went about it.

They skirted the bulkhead of the main air tank. They headed along the broader corridor which went past the indented inner door of the air lock. They had reached that indentation when Baird saw that the inner airlock door was closing. He saw a human pressure suit past its edge. He saw the corner of some object that had been put down on the air-lock floor.

Baird shouted, and rushed toward the lock. He seized the inner handle and tried to force open the door again, so that no one inside it could emerge into the emptiness without. He failed. He wrenched frantically at the control of the outer door. It suddenly swung freely. The outer door had been put on manual. It could be and was being opened from inside.

"Tell the skipper," raged Baird. "Taine's taking something out!" He tore open a pressure-suit cupboard in the wall beside the lock door. "He'll make the Plumies think it's a return-gift for the generator!" He eeled into the pressure suit and zipped it up to his neck. "The man's crazy! He thinks we can take their ship and stay alive for a while! Dammit, our air would ruin half their equipment! Tell the skipper to send help!"

He wrenched at the door again, jamming down his helmet with one hand. And this time the control worked. Taine, most probably, had forgotten that the inner control was disengaged only when the manual was actively in use. Diane raced away, panting. Baird swore bitterly at the slowness of the outer door's closing. He was tearing at the inner door long before it could be opened. He flung himself in and dragged it shut, and struck the emergency air-release which bled the air lock into space for speed of operation. He thrust out the outer door and plunged through.

His momentum carried him almost too far. He fell, and only the magnetic soles of his shoes enabled him to check himself. He was in that singular valley between the two ships, where their hulls were impregnably welded fast. Round-hulled Plumie ship, and ganoid-shaped *Niccola*, they stuck immovably together as if they had been that way since time began. Where the sky appeared above Baird's head, the stars moved in stately procession across the valley roof.

He heard a metallic rapping through the fabric of his space armor. Then sunlight glittered, and the valley filled with a fierce glare, and a man in a human spacesuit stood on the *Niccola's* plating, opposite the Plumie air lock. He held a bulky object under his arm. With his other gauntlet he rapped again.

"You fool!" shouted Baird. "Stop that! We couldn't use their ship, anyhow!"

His space phone had turned on with the air supply. Taine's voice snarled:

"We'll try! You keep back! They are not human!"

But Baird ran toward him. The sensation of running upon magnetic-soled shoes was unearthly: it was like trying to run on fly-paper or bird-lime. But in addition there was no gravity here, and no sense of balance, and there was the feeling of perpetual fall.

There could be no science nor any skill in an encounter under such conditions. Baird partly ran and partly staggered and partly skated to where Taine faced him, snarling. He threw himself at the other man—and then the sun vanished behind the bronze ship's hull, and only stars moved visibly in all the universe.

But the sound of his impact was loud in Baird's ears inside the suit. There was a slightly different sound when his armor struck Taine's, and when it struck the heavier metal of the two ships. He fought. But the suits were intended to be defense against greater stresses than human blows could offer. In the darkness, it was like two blindfolded men fighting each other while encased in pillows.

Then the sun returned, floating sedately above the valley, and Baird could see his enemy. He saw, too, that the Plumie air lock was now open and that a small, erect, and somehow jaunty figure in golden space armor stood in the opening and watched gravely as the two men fought.

Taine cursed, panting with hysterical hate. He flung himself at Baird, and Baird toppled because he'd put one foot past the welded boundary between the *Niccola's* cobalt steel and the Plumie ship's bronze. One foot held to nothing. And that was a ghastly sensation, because if Taine only tugged his other foot free and heaved—why—then Baird would go floating away from the rotating, now-twinned ships, floating farther and farther away forever.

But darkness fell, and he scrambled back to the *Niccola's* hull as a disorderly parade of stars went by above him. He pantingly waited fresh attack. He felt something—and it was the object Taine had meant to offer as a return present to the Plumies. It was unquestionably explosive, either booby-trapped or timed to explode inside the Plumie ship. Now it rocked gently, gripped by the magnetism of the steel.

The sun appeared again, and Taine was yards away, crawling and fumbling for Baird. Then he saw him, and rose and rushed, and the clankings of his shoe-soles were loud. Baird flung himself at Taine in a savage tackle.

He struck Taine's legs a glancing blow, and the cobalt steel held his armor fast, but Taine careened and bounced against the round bronze wall of the Plumie, and bounced again. Then he screamed, because he went floating slowly out to emptiness, his arms and legs jerking spasmodically, while he shrieked . . .

The Plumie in the air lock stepped out. He trailed a cord behind him. He leaped briskly toward nothingness.

There came quick darkness once more, and Baird struggled erect despite the adhesiveness of the *Niccola's* hull. When he was fully upright, sick with horror at what had come about, there was sunlight yet again, and men were coming out of the *Niccola's* air lock, and the Plumie who'd leaped for space was pulling himself back to his own ship

33

again. He had a loop of the cord twisted around Taine's leg. But Taine screamed and screamed inside his spacesuit.

It was odd that one could recognize the skipper even inside space armor. But Baird felt sick. He saw Taine received, still screaming, and carried into the lock. The skipper growled an infuriated demand for details. His space phone had come on, too, when its air supply began. Baird explained, his teeth chattering.

"*Hah!*" grunted the skipper. "*Taine was a mistake. He shouldn't ever have left ground. When a man's potty in one fashion, there'll be cracks in him all over. What's this?*"

The Plumie in the golden armor very soberly offered the skipper the object Taine had meant to introduce into the Plumie's ship. Baird said desperately that he'd fought against it, because he believed it a booby trap to kill the Plumies so men could take their ship and fill it with air and cut it free, and then make a landing somewhere.

"*Damned foolishness!*" rumbled the skipper. "*Their ship'd begin to crumble with our air in it! If it held to a landing—*"

Then he considered the object he'd accepted from the Plumie. It could have been a rocket war head, enclosed in some container that would detonate it if opened. Or there might be a timing device. The skipper grunted. He heaved it skyward.

The misshapen object went floating away toward emptiness. Sunlight smote harshly upon it.

"*Don't want it back in the* Niccola," growled the skipper, "*but just to make sure—*"

He fumbled a hand weapon out of his belt. He raised it, and it spurted flame—very tiny blue-white sparks, each one indicating a pellet of metal flung away at high velocity.

One of them struck the shining, retreating container. It exploded with a monstrous, soundless, violence. It had been a rocket's war head. There could have been only one reason for it to be introduced into a Plumie ship. Baird ceased to be shaky. Instead, he was ashamed.

The skipper growled inarticulately. He looked at the Plumie, again standing in the golden ship's air lock.

"*We'll go back, Mr. Baird. What you've done won't save our lives, and nobody will ever know you did it. But I think well of you. Come along!*"

This was at 11 hours 5 minutes ship time.

A good half hour later the skipper's voice bellowed from the speakers all over the *Niccola*. His heavy-jowled features stared doggedly out of screens wherever men were on duty or at ease.

"*Hear this!*" he said forbiddingly. "*We have checked our course and speed. We have verified that there is no possible jury-rig for our engines that could get us into any sort of orbit, let alone land us on the only planet in this system with air we could breathe. It is officially certain that in thirteen days nine hours from now, the* Niccola *will be so close to the sun that her hull will melt down. Which will be no loss to us because we'll be dead then, still going on into the sun to be vaporized with the ship. There is nothing to be done about it. We can do nothing to save our own lives!*"

He glared out of each and every one of the screens, wherever there were men to see him.

"*But,*" he rumbled, "*the Plumies can get away if we help them. They have no cutting torches. We have. We can cut their ship free. They can repair their drive—but it's most likely that it'll operate perfectly when they're a mile from the* Niccola's *magnetic field. They can't help us. But we can help them. And sooner or later some Plumie ship is going to encounter some other human ship. If we cut these Plumies loose, they'll report what we did. When they meet other men, they'll be cagey because they'll remember Taine. But they'll know they can make friends, because we did them a favor when we'd nothing to gain by it. I can offer no reward. But I ask for volunteers to go outside and cut the Plumie ship loose, so the Plumies can go home in safety instead of on into the sun with us!*"

He glared, and cut off the image.

Diane held tightly to Baird's hand, in the radar room. He said evenly:

"There'll be volunteers. The Plumies are pretty sporting characters—putting up a fight with an unarmed ship, and so on. If there aren't enough other volunteers, the skipper and I will cut them free by ourselves."

Diane said, dry-throated:

"I'll help. So I can be with you. We've got—so little time."

"I'll ask the skipper as soon as the Plumie ship's free."

"Y-yes," said Diane. And she pressed her face against his shoulder, and wept.

This was at 01 hours, 20 minutes ship time. At 03 hours even, there was peculiar activity in the valley between the welded ships. There were men in space armor working cutting-torches where for twenty feet the two ships were solidly attached. Blue-white flames bored savagely into solid metal, and melted copper gave off strangely colored clouds of vapor—which emptiness whisked away to nothing—and molten iron and cobalt made equally lurid clouds of other colors.

There were Plumies in the air lock, watching.

At 03 hours 40 minutes ship time, all the men but one drew back. They went inside the *Niccola*. Only one man remained, cutting at the last sliver of metal that held the two ships together.

It parted. The Plumie ship swept swiftly away, moved by the centrifugal force of the rotary motion the joined vessels had possessed. It dwindled and dwindled. It was a half mile away A mile. The last man on the outside of the *Niccola's* hull thriftily brought his torch to the air lock and came in.

Suddenly, the distant golden hull came to life. It steadied. It ceased to spin, however slowly. It darted ahead. It checked. It swung to the right and left and up and down. It was alive again.

In the radar room, Diane walked into Baird's arms and said shakily:

"Now we . . . we have almost fourteen days."

"Wait," he commanded. "When the Plumies understood what we were doing, and why, they drew diagrams. They hadn't thought of cutting free, out in space, without the spinning saws they used to cut bronze with. But they asked for a scanner and a screen. They checked on its use. I want to see—"

He flipped on the screen. And there was instantly a Plumie looking eagerly out of it, for some sign of communication established. There were soprano sounds, and he waved a hand for attention. Then he zestfully held up one diagram after another.

Baird drew a deep breath. A very deep breath. He pressed the navigation-room call. The skipper looked dourly at him.

"*Well?*" said the skipper forbiddingly.

"Sir," said Baird, very quietly indeed, "the Plumies are talking by diagram over the communicator set we gave them. Their drive works. They're as well off as they ever were. And they've been modifying their tractor beams—stepping them up to higher power."

"*What of it?*" demanded the skipper, rumbling.

"They believe," said Baird, "that they can handle the *Niccola* with their beefed-up tractor beams." He wetted his lips. "They're going to tow us to the oxygen planet ahead, sir. They're going to set us down on it. They'll help us find the metals we need to build the tools to repair the *Niccola*, sir. You see the reasoning, sir. We turned them loose to improve

36

the chance of friendly contact when another human ship runs into them. They want us to carry back—to be proof that Plumies and men can be friends. It seems that—they like us, sir."

He stopped for a moment. Then he went on reasonably;

"And besides that, it'll be one hell of a fine business proposition. We never bother with hydrogen-methane planets. They've minerals and chemicals we haven't got, but even the stones of a methane-hydrogen planet are ready to combine with the oxygen we need to breathe! We can't carry or keep enough oxygen for real work. The same thing's true with them on an oxygen planet. We can't work on each other's planets, but we can do fine business in each other's minerals and chemicals from those planets. I've got a feeling, sir, that the Plumie cairns are location-notices; markers set up over ore deposits they can find but can't hope to work, yet they claim against the day when their scientists find a way to make them worth owning. I'd be willing to bet, sir, that if we explored hydrogen planets as thoroughly as oxygen ones, we'd find cairns on their-type planets that they haven't colonized yet."

The skipper stared. His mouth dropped open.

"And I think, sir," said Baird, "that until they detected us they thought they were the only intelligent race in the galaxy. They were upset to discover suddenly that they were not, and at first they'd no idea what we'd be like. But I'm guessing now, sir, that they're figuring on what chemicals and ores to start swapping with us." Then he added, "When you think of it, sir, probably the first metal they ever used was aluminum—where our ancestors used copper—and they had a beryllium age next, instead of iron. And right now, sir, it's probably as expensive for them to refine iron as it is for us to handle titanium and beryllium and osmium—which are duck soup for them! Our two cultures ought to thrive as long as we're friends, sir. They know it already—and we'll find it out in a hurry!"

The skipper's mouth moved. It closed, and then dropped open again. The search for the Plumies had been made because it looked like they had to be fought. But Baird had just pointed out some extremely commonsense items which changed the situation entirely. And there was evidence that the Plumies saw the situation the new way. The skipper felt such enormous relief that his manner changed. He displayed what was almost effusive cordiality—for the skipper. He cleared his throat.

"*Hm-m-m. Hah! Very good, Mr. Baird,*" he said formidably. *"And of course with time and air and metals we can re-build our drive. For that matter, we could rebuild the* Niccola! *I'll notify the ship's company, Mr. Baird. Very good!"* He moved to use another microphone. Then he checked himself. *"Your expression is odd, Mr. Baird. Did you wish to say something more?"*

"Y-yes, sir," said Baird. He held Diane's hand fast. "It'll be months before we get back to port, sir. And it's normally against regulations, but under the circumstances . . . would you mind . . . as skipper . . . marrying Lieutenant Holt and me?"

The skipper snorted. Then he said almost—almost—amiably?

"Hm-m-m. You've both done very well, Mr. Baird. Yes. Come to the navigation room and we'll get it over with. Say—ten minutes from now."

Baird grinned at Diane. Her eyes shone a little.

This was at 04 hours 10 minutes ship time. It was exactly twelve hours since the alarm-bell rang.

Fugitive from Space

WHEN the first streaks of light appeared among the stars, Burt was telling Norma goodnight. He had left the motor of his car running as earnest of his intention to leave imme-diately, but he didn't want to go. This was up at Lake Ka-tona, where he'd borrowed a lakeside cottage to get some writing done. Norma happened to be vacationing at a board-ing-house at the same resort, and they'd met and it seemed very remarkable. They even discovered that they lived with-in blocks of each other when not on vacation, though they'd never met. Burt discovered to his astonishment that he even knew the building in which Norma had a small apartment. So it was very plainly an act of destiny, no less, which caused them to encounter each other here.

The sky was like velvet. Night-insects whirred insistently. The scents of summer filled the air. There was no moon.

"Maybe tomorrow," said Burt, reluctantly ready to depart, "tomorrow we can—"

Then the first streak of light flashed across the sky.

It wasn't a shooting-star. It wasn't even a streak of light, but a tiny spot of lurid brightness, which shone so harshly and moved so swiftly that it seemed to be a line.

There was another flash. They saw it clearly. The glow it left behind was sharp-edged. It looked like a line-wide strip of the Milky Way stretched across the sky.

"I don't know what it is," admitted Burt. "I've never seen anything like it before."

A third spot of brightness flashed from somewhere to westward. A fourth streak. It was straight. A fifth. The sixth made a parabolic dash across the sky. The seventh—

Then other lights appeared. Five of them. They appeared arbitrarily to the north and south and west and snapped across the firmament—leaving trails of luminosity behind them—until they joined where the motionless new flare glowed. That flare burst violently, without any sound whatever. For one instant it was brighter than sunlight. Then it turned yellow, faded swiftly to orange, and went out in an infinitesimal speck of red which ceased to be.

Six lights like small lurid stars moved restlessly about the place where it had been. They left glowing trails behind them. Then, in quick random succession, they winked out.

There was stillness. Silence, save for the idling of the motor of Burt's car and the night-insects and the faint rustle of the wind in the trees. Then there were voices. A long distance away, somebody shouted to somebody else. There had been that flash of really extraordinary brightness, and wakeful people had noted it. Perhaps some people were waked by it. Many came to their windows to see its cause. They looked skyward, and saw the meaningless hieroglyphic in the heavens.

Burt and Norma still stared upward. Norma whispered:

"Do you—suppose that was—near?"

Burt shrugged. "I think it was in our atmosphere, yes. That first line is getting blurry. And I think all the lines are moving a little. There's a bright star there, shining right through one of those lines. A moment ago it was outside it."

He was right. The pattern in the sky was shifting, though very slowly. Also it was blurring. Where Burt stood, there were voices all about. Somebody called authoritatively:

"Vapor-trails! They're the vapor-trails of jet-planes up there! Night maneuvers!"

Burt shook his head a little. Norma whispered again.

"Is it that, Burt? Vapor-trails from planes?"

"They wouldn't show at night," said Burt, "unless in bright moonlight, and there isn't any moon. No: Planes didn't make those lines! And what exploded?"

"What?" asked Norma.

"I don't know. I'm asking." Burt continued to frown upward.

People came out of the boarding-houses, pulling on wraps and bathrobes to stare up at the heavens. None had seen the lights themselves. Most had looked out because of the flashing, noiseless explosion in mid-sky which had lighted all the world for part of a second. They'd seen the streaks of luminosity. Now they came out to gape at them.

But nothing happened. Burt's car-engine purred quietly. People called to each other. There was that curious gaiety which overtakes commonplace human beings when something happens which is startling enough to justify unconventional behavior or attire.

Norma drew away from Burt.

"The lines are fading," said Burt awkwardly. "I guess I'll be going. See you tomorrow?"

She nodded. She pressed his hand and moved toward the door. Burt got in his car and drove away. There were many people out-of-doors now, with blankets or shawls about their nightclothing. They continued to call to each other. Apparently all had been roused by the flash of light from something which had appeared to explode. Apparently nobody else had seen the spots of light which had made the now blurring lines among the stars.

The lakeside village ended. Burt drove along the narrow concrete highway that circled the lake and served the cottages and small estates upon its shores. The windows of his car were open, and all the fragrance of the night blew through. The highway curved and curved. There were trees. There were the ditches beside the road. Now and again a mailbox. Once or twice more elaborate gateways. The elaboration of entrances was not always proportionate to the buildings inside them. The smell of pine-tags. Once or twice, dim lights in houses well back from the road.

Ahead, there was a clearing where somebody had cut down trees to make room for a summer cottage and a lawn. A toolshed showed in the headlight beams. Burt knew that there was a pile of building material a little way back in the open space. His car came out of the trees. He leaned forward to look up through the windshield at the dimming pattern in the sky.

The stars were blotted out. Something huge and black was plunging down. It was close.

It was upon him.

Brownish leathery stuff descended before the car and cut off its headlight-beams. It descended on both sides. The car was in a tent of unlikely brown flexible material. There were many cords and ropes. Something bulky writhed and struggled. . . .

Then the car's front wheels ran over the edge of the fabric which had dropped about it. There were many strainings. The front wheels took charge. They tried to ride up the fabric side-walls. The fabric should have ripped. It did not. There was a chaotic, nightmarish instant in which the car plunged frantically in a confusion of resistant stuff. If Burt had driven headlong into the open end of a canvas tent with a floor-cloth, and if the material were so strong the car couldn't breast its way through, the feel of things would have been similar.

The ending might have been similar, too. The car reeled over on its side, skidding sickishly on its rear wheels. Burt struggled frantically to steer. Somehow he knew that something else that was alive struggled as frantically as himself.

Then the car overturned and his head hit something solid. He slid into unconsciousness.

Later he had a moment of vague half-consciousness in which his sensations were completely impossible. His brain felt cold. There was a feeling of chill, of frigidity, inside his mind. Not on the skin or flesh of his skull, but inside! Which of course could not be.

He was thinking absorbedly about the cottage by the lake, and a picture of the cottage flashed through his mind, and he remembered all its rooms as empty, and then he remembered in detail the way to the cottage, and where he turned off on his own driveway, and exactly how to open the door with his key. And he was vaguely bewildered that he was thinking of such things, because he knew that he wanted to find out what had fallen on his car and what had happened to him. But his mind would not work the way he wanted it to. It refused to function normally.

Then it stopped working altogether. He was unconscious again.

He ached all over and his eyes were bandaged when he came back to himself. He heard the chirping of birds. It would be daytime again. He heard somebody moving about in the next room. The covers were tight about his body. He stirred. He knew that all his members responded but there were sundry hurtings that told him he was bruised. His eyes, though—

41

He felt a twinge of panic. He struggled to raise his arms to touch the bandage that blinded him.

There was a crash beside the bed. Somebody came running. A voice said:

"Easy, there! Hold everything."

Burt felt himself gently pressed down in the bed again. The voice was masculine and completely familiar, but he couldn't recognize it. It confused and bewildered him.

"Easy!" repeated the voice. Its intonation was matter-of-fact. "You got banged up a little last night. I'm looking after you. You'll be all right. Just lie still a little while longer."

"My—eyes!" panted Burt. They felt all right, but they were bandaged! He sweated in apprehension that he had been blinded.

"Don't worry," said the voice, without emotion. "Just hold everything for half an hour and you can get up."

Burt felt himself held fast. Gently, but he couldn't move. He said shakily:

"Who are you?"

"Smith," said the voice. "John Smith. You don't know me. I'm just looking after you until the doctor gets back and says you can get up. I found you last night."

The voice was incredibly familiar. He'd heard it over and over again. He recognized it, absolutely. But he didn't know anybody named John Smith. Certainly not anybody who could talk to him in a voice as familiar to him as his own—

Then he did know whose the voice was. He gasped. He knew he was wide-awake, but his just-discovered knowledge was as much like a nightmare as anything could possibly be. He wavered precariously between an hysterically violent reaction, and a paralysis of pure horror. This was insanity! He must be insane! He must be!

The completely known voice said:

"Look, Burt! You just promise to lie still here until the doctor comes, and everything'll be all right."

Burt knew that he was deathly white. He felt that way. He lay still, numb with horror. The voice said:

"Okay? You'll do that?"

Burt didn't move or answer. He couldn't. He was stunned by the recognition of the voice. He seemed, probably, to have fainted. There was a moment's silence, and then a readjustment of the bedclothing over him. It tightened. The footsteps went into the next room. And Burt would have done something completely insane if he'd recognized them. But they were not familiar footsteps. The door stayed open. Burt lay absolutely motionless. He was thinking crazily that this couldn't be, and if it was he was out of his head. Because he knew, now, whose voice it was. It was perfectly reasonable that he shouldn't have recognized it at first. Now he did. But it was impossible!

The voice that had spoken to him was his own.

His own voice had called him Burt. His own voice had told him to keep still until the doctor came. And then he, using his own voice, had asked questions, and his own voice in another throat had put him off.

Frozen, he heard small movements in the next room. He stirred with infinite caution—the cunning of the insane, he thought desperately. The cover was tight across his shoulders. When he'd moved, before, something crashed to the floor. One side of the cover was tucked tightly under the mattress. The other must be laid flat on a chair with something heavy on it. When he stirred, that heavy thing would be upset.

With infinite, frantic care he moved his right arm sidewise, not loosening the cover at all. He brought his hand up past his shoulder, flat to the mattress, and turned his face to it. He fumbled at the bandage over his eyes and plucked it away. He could see. There was nothing wrong with his eyesight. There were no scratches from broken glass or anything else about his face. He saw the end of the cover resting on the chair beside his bed. It was devised exactly as he'd expected, so that movement which loosened the cover would pull the bucket on it, and the bucket would fall. It was to give notice when he moved.

But it was easy to defeat. A lunatic could defeat it. Burt had merely to loosen the cover at the other side of the bed, where the mattress held it. He did. He was in his pajamas. He had evidently been put carefully to bed while unconscious.

He got up very quietly, though his teeth tended to chatter. There were noises in the room nearest the lake. This John Smith was doing something there. Burt picked up the bucket as a weapon. It should have been an alarm. He wasn't sure why he wanted a weapon, because outside the sun shone and birds sang very peacefully, but Burt was in a precarious psychological state. Somebody had blindfolded him and tried to persuade him he was seriously injured. But it was worse than that! The somebody who'd deceived him about his eyes was using Burt's own voice to lie to him with. And Burt felt a crawling horror at that thought.

But he went very softly to the door and peered into the next room.

43

There was a figure seated in a chair at his own worktable. The figure wore one of his shirts, and a pair of his trousers, and his shoes. It was bent over something at which it labored. There were yards and yards of leathery brónze-color stuff— not woven fabric—in a heap at one side of the room. The figure was working with pieces cut out of it.

Burt found rage choking him. It was necessary to rage, or he would be frightened. But then the figure's hands lifted something. Burt saw what it was. It was a face, modeled in the leathery material. But it was flexible. It was like a child's rubber-latex Hallowe'en mask, save that it was not grotesque and was of the unchanged bronze color of its substance. But it was remarkably flexible. It yielded in the figure's hands.

The figure put the face on itself.

Burt made a strangled noise. The figure started up and faced him. It wore the face Burt had just seen in its hands.

And Burt knew the truth, then. He couldn't have put it into words, but it filled him with a sickish horror past all reason. It wasn't even a relief to know that he wasn't crazy. He wanted to be sick. He wanted to explode in murderous fury. He wanted to kill. In fact, a part of his horror came from astonishment that he hadn't been killed—that he was alive and looking at what he looked at.

Then his own voice spoke matter-of-factly from across the room. "It looks like you've guessed."

Burt heard words come out of his own mouth. "It was —those lights in the sky," he said thickly. "You!"

The figure seemed to reflect. Then it nodded.

"And the thing I ran into," panted Burt absurdly, "with the car. That was you landing—with a parachute." His voice in his own throat was strange—and it was good for it to be so. It was unlike the voice of the figure. "You—fell on my car."

The figure said matter-of-factly:

"Yes. I was landing."

"You—you're not a man!" said Burt thickly. "You're not —human!"

"No."

There was a pause. The figure stood and looked at him. Burt felt an ache in his fingers. He had gripped the door-frame so tightly that his whole hand hurt. He loosened it. Then he said in ridiculous vexation:

"But you're wearing my clothes. You talk English!" Then he found himself angry despite his horror. "You're talking with my voice! You've got a hell of a nerve!"

The figure paused. Then it said tonelessly:

"I am a fugitive. I had no clothes like you wear. So I took yours. I planned to hide in the woods when I had finished this face."

"That's not your face, either!" raged Burt. "You copied it from a picture on my work-table! But it isn't colored right. How'd you get my voice? What the hell do you mean, anyhow?"

He listened to his own complaints, amazed at their irrelevance. But one does not react with calm and reasoned thoughts in the face of the unthinkable as a visible and patent fact. He saw the figure spread out its hands as if somehow it knew that that was an appropriate gesture.

"I was a fugitive," it repeated without any intonation whatever. "I was being chased. I reached your atmosphere. My pursuers were close. I set my ship to go on by itself and I jumped. My pursuers caught my ship and destroyed it. They searched with their—" a pause here—"weapons for me. But I had jumped in time. They did not find me. They may believe I was in my ship when they destroyed it. But they will try to make sure. Therefore I must hide."

Burt's mind went dizzily in several directions at once. A picture in a magazine on the work-table, that was the model for the face. His voice and the use of English he couldn't understand. And there was the fact that this figure had admitted that it was not a human being. But it was intelligent! It was rational!

It happens that the idea of non-human intelligence is the most horrifying of possible concepts. The idea of a non-human which thinks and talks is the idea of a demon, a ghost, a werewolf, a monster, a devil out of hell. Burt's hair tended to stand on end.

But on the other hand the creature spoke tonelessly, without attempts either to frighten or persuade. It described flight and pursuit and escape. The flashing lights in the sky, last night, and the incredible soundless explosion Burt had seen, were points which checked with its story. But they added up to the statement that Burt was faced in his own living room with a fugitive from space—a member of a race so far beyond men in science or intelligence that they had ships which roamed the stars, and weapons whose nature Burt could guess at.

He sat down abruptly in a chair.

"L-look," he said shakily. "This is—impossible, of course, but all the same . . ."

The figure waited. After a moment it said:

45

"I did not expect to talk to humans so soon. I thought to have my disguise complete and to be hiding in the woods before you woke. Then you would have been puzzled, and you would be angry, but you would not have seen me." Then the figure said as tonelessly as before: "I have much to think of and plan."

"If—you're on the run," said Burt jerkily. "It's important that nobody knows you're here and alive?"

"If I am known to have landed, I will be destroyed," said the figure in that extraordinarily prosaic manner. "My pursuers may have ways of learning if my landing is known. I do not know. If they do learn I am alive, they will destroy me even if they have to destroy this world to make sure of it."

Burt said querulously:

"But what do you mean to do?"

"I mean to hide, so your radios will not speak of me or your newspapers know that I exist."

"And after?"

There was a pause as if the creature sought for a gesture or a word that fitted. It shrugged.

"I am on your world not of my own choice. I may never be able to leave it. I have to think."

The figure stood quite unnaturally still and looked at Burt. And he was horrified and repelled, but he was also tormented with curiosity and not wholly capable of coherent thought. He was not sure he believed the alien's story, but nobody else would believe in the alien's existence. He needed to do some thinking himself.

"I could do with a chance to think too," said Burt uneasily. "I take it you've told me this much because you don't want me to tell anybody you're here until you've had time to make some decisions."

The figure nodded its head.

"I'm pretty dizzy," Burt told him," but I know well enough that if I tried to persuade anybody that a man from Mars— or wherever you're from—had paid me a visit, they'd lock me up. I think you're safe from babbling on my part! But I'm not too clear-headed just now. Suppose you go off in the woods and do your thinking. Come back here tonight. We'll talk things over, then, when we both are able to—have a little perspective on it. Right?"

He desperately wanted the creature to get out of his sight just now. He wanted to be in a normal world when he thought about incredible things. He still did not quite believe his eyes and ears.

The figure—it had the build of an athletic man, and Burt's clothes fitted it rather well—prosaically began to make a bundle of the plastic brown material from which it had made itself a face and hands, and very probably other elements of a humanoid body as well. But it moved deftly enough. It made a surprisingly small bundle of the fabric that had been its parachute. It moved to the door. Then it paused.

"I should tell you," said the figure tonelessly, "that I have the usual emergency weapons of my race. I will not allow myself to be made a captive. If necessary, I can explode what you call an atom bomb."

Burt's mouth dropped open. The figure nodded carefully, as if conscious that this was the proper gesture to make. It reached inside Burt's shirt, which it was wearing. It brought out a small, misshapen metal object. It showed the object to Burt and put it away again and went out of the door. Through the window Burt saw it move away toward the woods.

Birds sang loudly in the sunshine.

Norma was at the swimming-place when Burt found her. All the summer boarders and people whose cottages did not front on the lake came to the incorporated village for their swimming. There were diving-boards and diving-towers, a fenced-off shallow area for small children, and spaces and facilities where lovers of the out-of-doors in summer could anoint themselves with sun-tan oil, wear dark glasses, and make acquaintances if they hadn't any, and snub unneeded acquaintances if they had. The lake was a very normal sort of vacation resort.

Today the sky was beautifully blue, and there were cotton-wool clouds in the sky. There were squealings and laughter from those who swam in the lake, and there was a humming of talk from those who sat at tables and drank soft drinks and either took pleasure in the act, or else enjoyed themselves by pretending to be bored. Everything was quite appropriate for the pleasure of people temporarily without cares.

Norma splashed cheerfully to shore when Burt arrived.

"Aren't you swimming?" she asked in surprise.

He shook his head, speechless. She swung up to the platform and sat there, dripping and with the sunlight shining on her wetted skin. She regarded him with her head cocked on one side.

"You sounded queer this morning," she observed. "All you said was yes and no. Even when I told you I'd be here."

47

"I sounded queer—" Burt tensed. "You talked to me?"

"Naturally!" said Norma. "You remember! I phoned that a gang was going on a picnic and that we'd stop at your cottage for you if you'd go. All you said was no. Then I said I didn't care much about the picnic, myself, and would you be along here, and you said yes." She looked at his face and flushed. She said awkwardly: "I didn't really care about the picnic."

Burt found his hands clenched tightly.

"You weren't talking to me," he said in a strangled voice.

"But I was!" Then Norma stopped short. She said with some constraint. "I—the last thing you said last night was something about today. That's why I called. I misunderstood, I guess."

She moved to slip overboard again, but Burt said:

"Hold it!" He swallowed. "It wasn't me you talked to. It was somebody—" He hesitated. The figure wearing his clothes and using his voice was not exactly a somebody, but a something. He went on, "It was somebody who sounded like me, pretending to be me. I didn't know you telephoned. I . . ."

Then his voice failed him. In this particular place, with such completely ordinary activities all about, it struck him very forcibly indeed that what had happened last night and this morning was not exactly credible.

"L-look," he said unsteadily. "I was certain I wasn't crazy, just now, but what I remember is! Come along a moment, will you?"

He led the way from the swimming-space to his car. Norma followed, stepping carefully in her bare feet. Burt's teeth chattered suddenly. He pointed to the mud-guards of his car. They were bent but not scratched.

"On the way to the cottage last night," said Burt constrainedly, "after I left you, I ran into something. The car turned over. You can see the dents."

Norma stared, and turned to him in quick concern:

"Burt! Were you hurt?"

He looked at the dents. There was not a single scratch on the paint. The leathery stuff, of course, had not prevented denting, but it had protected the paint against abrasion.

"Did you ever see dents like those?" he demanded. "It looks as if there'd been something like a cloth protecting the paint when the dents were made, doesn't it?"

"Why, yes," agreed Norma. "What happened?"

He told her about something huge and dark falling swiftly

from the sky and overwhelming the car. Sweat stood out on his forehead. There were people all about. There were the half-dozen stores of the village, with perfectly commonplace customers going in and out of them. There was everyday sunshine and trees looked as they had always looked. People ate hot dogs, and children consumed ice-cream cones, and back at the water's edge a squealing, laughing struggle took place as somebody tried to push somebody else overboard, and there was a splash as both contestants fell into the water together. It was completely natural and commonplace. Burt's story seemed inconceivable in such a setting. He stopped the tale at the point where he'd been knocked unconscious.

Norma stared at him, paling. Droplets of lake-water still stood on her tanned skin. She was the only human being to whom Burt would have dared tell even so much, though he had known her only a week. But she had seen the lights in the sky, last night, and anyhow it is possible to feel remarkably close to a person like Norma in a week.

"Does that sound crazy?" he demanded when he'd finished.

She shook her head.

"Did you see the morning paper?" she asked in turn. "It said that there were stories of streaks of light in the sky last night. It said that phenomena like northern lights were rare as far south as this, but that they aren't unknown. I wondered if the lights we saw were auroral displays. But from what *you* say . . ."

"They weren't," said Burt.

"Then the thing that fell out of the sky on your car . . ."

"If you'll get dressed," he told her, "I'll show you where it happened. It came from a ship up there. Maybe it was a hundred miles high, at the very edge of the atmosphere. But there was a ship. —I'm going to make a phone call," he added abruptly. "Maybe I can find out something useful. Meet me here?"

She smiled at him quickly and moved away. Just as a man can find it possible to tell a girl his inmost and most private thoughts after knowing her only a week, a girl can find possible the most unquestioning obedience, within limits, in a similar length of time.

Burt made the phone-call. He was back at the parked car when Norma came out, immaculate though her hair was wetted a 'little where the edge of her swimming-cap had been. He opened the cardoor in silence. He started the motor and backed out from the curb.

"I just telephoned the FBI, long-distance," he told her. "I said I was a science-fiction writer, asking for information."

"Why?"

"If you say you're a writer," he said detachedly, "it's expected that the information you ask for will be on the wacky side. And you get all sorts of cooperation. It works anywhere. I told the FBI I was working on a story and explained that the character in my yarn needed to convince the FBI that he had encountered an alien from outer space. And I asked what sort of evidence he'd need, to appear somebody who wasn't a crackpot telling a story that shouldn't be true. Fellow at the FBI office gave me some good advice on how to make the thing convincing. Said to let him know when the yarn was printed."

Norma frowned a little. "Encountered . . ."

"Yes," said Burt grimly. "I'm going to try to find proof to convince the FBI that I did encounter a creature from another world, who landed on Earth from a space-ship. I did. The thing that dropped on my car was a parachute, and a creature was in it."

Driving out of the village, he told her the rest of his story —from the instant he waked in his own bed, blindfolded, until the creature that spoke with his own voice went away —so it said—to hide in the woods until nightfall.

"I told it it needn't fear my talking," added Burt coldly, "because nobody would believe me. I didn't really believe it myself. How could a creature tumbling down out of the sky speak English? But no actual man could duplicate my voice! Something happened, and the only plausible guess happens to be lunatic. So I'm going to try to get evidence to convince the FBI—whose business it would be to handle anything as important as possible information about space-travel —and let them take over from there. I don't want any part of the business for myself!"

Norma shivered a little. But she said quietly:

"If you were—abnormal, Burt, you wouldn't be willing to allow for doubt. You'd resent anybody not believing you. But instead you act just the way a person should when up against something that's been thought impossible."

"Thanks," said Burt drily.

He drove. Norma frowned a little, beside him. He drove along the exact way he'd followed the night before. The highway curved and curved, encircling the lake. There were trees which thickened into woodland through which the car rolled. There were little driveways branching off, with mail-boxes at the turnoffs. They led to the lake-shore cottages. There was the aromatic smell of pines, and the sound of insects, and there were faint, faint birdcalls, and now and again a shingled cottage with an encircling screened porch.

Burt pulled off to the side of the road and stopped the car. He got out. Norma joined him. He said grimly:

"These marks—" he pointed— "are where I went off the road. There's no pattern of the tread, because my tires were running on that brown stuff I told you about. The parachute. Here's where the car turned over."

In the soft mould the mark of the car's toppled body was clear. There were leaves and twigs pressed flat. There was the cut-off stump of a six-inch tree. It was plainly the thing that had made the deepest dent in the car.

"The car turned over all right, you see," said Burt. "Now, how did it get turned back on its wheels?"

He searched. Presently he pointed, without saying a word. There were two deep indentations in the soft earth. If a man were strong enough to lift at the side of a toppled light car, and set it upright again, the place where he planted his feet would show deep footmarks from the weight. But not many human beings could do such a thing as had been done with Burt's car.

On the other hand, these weren't human footprints.

Norma shivered a little.

"Unfortunately," said Burt coldly, "there's no detail. Maybe the creature was wearing something on the order of shoes."

He hesitated a moment. Then he said frowning:

"I'm pretty well convinced I'm not crazy, Norma. Especially since you don't seem to think I am. But I'm going to need evidence to convince the FBI that I'm not cracked. And there's the fact that if things go right I'll want you to back my story of the lights in the sky—but if they go wrong I want you away from here. Well away from here! That's important."

Norma said uneasily:

"You're thinking of what it said about an atom bomb?"

He nodded.

"But Burt," she said more uneasily still. "You don't *want* to be involved in this! It isn't really your affair. If you decided to finish your vacation somewhere else, couldn't you just drop the whole matter?"

He shook his head.

"There's a slight patriotic obligation," he said drily. "The

51

creature came here in a space-ship. Its pursuers were after it in other space-ships. They had weapons which apparently broke down air into atomic flame, and when they hit this creature's ship they disintegrated it. We humans, and specifically our own government, do not know how to make space-ships or weapons like that. This creature does. It would be good if our government found out how to make such things—from it."

Norma listened, unhappily.

"Another point of view," said Burt. "The thing's a fugitive. It's in danger from its pursuers, it says. Even more, it's in danger from humans. What do you think would happen if unwarned human beings discovered something that wasn't human going around among human-kind? They'd panic, at best. At worst they'd try to kill it out of pure fear. And it would defend itself. It has what it calls emergency weapons. It spoke of an atom bomb, which might be possible or might not." He spread out his hands. "I've got to prevent that if I can."

Norma said reluctantly:

"What are you going to do, then?"

"Take you to a safe place. Write out what I know. Leave it with you. Come back and try to get proof that'll satisfy the FBI that they'd better come along and make contact with the creature and make some sort of bargain with it. If there's an explosion or other unhappy events, you take my written account to the FBI anyhow. Understand?"

Norma's forehead creased.

"You'll lose a lot of time . . ." Then she said uneasily, "You arranged to meet it in your cottage after dark, Burt. It's hiding in the woods now. If you hope to find some proof in your cottage, why not go now, right away, while it's gone? If you do find anything, by nightfall you could have somebody convinced and back here with you."

It looked like a highly practical suggestion. It looked right. If even a scrap of proof of the creature's existence remained at the cottage, by nightfall he could have made contact with confidential branches of the government. He could be back with somebody prepared to offer protection and secrecy in exchange for the information the alien creature possessed. An atom bomb that a man could carry in his hand . . . the knowledge of space-drives and weapons it could give . . .

"I'll risk ten minutes at the cottage," said Burt slowly. "If I don't find anything then, I take you off somewhere and do as I said." He looked sharply at her. "Take you back to the village first?"

She shook her head. She wouldn't be much safer in the village, anyhow. He got back in the car and drove on past the clearing. The highway was still narrow. It meandered, and sometimes the lake was visible through trees, and sometimes it was not. They saw a newly-painted canoe turned upside down to let its coating dry. A row of bathing suits on a line.

He reached the turn-off to his own cottage. A bare hundred yards, and the lake was clearly visible. The house was exactly as he had left it. He turned the car completely about before he stopped the motor.

"For a quick getaway if we need it," he said curtly. "Wait here. If you hear voices, drive like mad for town—and keep going!"

But Norma, shivering, turned off the ignition and got out.

"I'm afraid of the idea of being alone," she said apologetically. "I'd rather come in too."

Burt opened the door. For an instant it seemed to him that he smelled a faint—a very faint—unfamiliar scent which was practically undetectable. He wrinkled his nostrils, and it was gone. He went quickly and grimly through every room. Empty. He opened drawers and closets, quickly. He came back to Norma.

"He's still hiding," said Burt, "and he didn't leave anything stored where I can find it. But he was working here."

He went to the work-table. He found half a dozen very tiny scraps of the brown plastic material. It was as thick as thick wrapping-paper, but as flexible as tissue. Yet when he tugged at it it seemed not to give at all. It would be enormously strong, because his car had not been able to tear it. And such strength with such inbelievable flexibility was impossible to human technology. Anything as strong as this——

"This will probably do," he said in satisfaction. "We've nothing like this!"

"L-let's go, then," said Norma. "I'm frightened, Burt."

They started for the door. A shadow moved outside. And Burt's own voice said tonelessly:

"Hold it."

The figure filled the exit. It was the alien. It stood in the doorway and, silhouetted so, it looked remarkably human. It had the masculine features of a magazine illustration. It wore Burt's clothing.

But suddenly it was appalling. It was ghastly. It was horrifying! When it opened its mouth, its teeth were brown. Its lips were of the same color as its forehead. It suddenly looked like a bronze statue intolerably alive and clothed and moving.

And it spoke tonelessly in Burt's own voice:

"That is Norma. You will have to tell me what you plan."

Norma shrank into Burt's arms, speechless. The face and lips and teeth which were all one color made the thing which called itself John Smith a visible impossibility, visibly unhuman and as monstrous to look at as the thing out of space which it happened to be.

It moved toward them, now. Its eyes did not blink. They were uncanny. Their fixed, unintermittent regard was terrifying.

Burt swung Norma behind him and faced the thing in a sort of fury.

"Dammit!" he cried fiercely. "You're scaring her!"

The figure said tonelessly:

"She would not be afraid of me if you had not told her what I am. Put her in a chair."

It continued to move forward. Burt experienced the startled realization that it expected him to get out of its way, just as a man expects a dog to make way. Norma shuddered uncontrollably at the nearer approach of the thing from space. She might scream if it approached too closely. Burt turned and seated her in the one easy chair the living room of the cottage contained. He stood protectively before her, bristling.

"What do you want?" he demanded. "What's the matter? Why'd you come back here before dark?"

The figure spoke, again without inflections. Its brown teeth and brown lips and brown tongue made it seem demoniac, as if a statue had become possessed by a demon which used it as a body.

"I have been examining the memories I took from your mind when your car turned over," it said in its flat voice. "I cannot know what you have thought, but I know what you have seen and heard and done up to the time I took your memories. I have been learning your language and your civilization from that information. And I reasoned that you would come and try to get proof that I have landed on this world. You should wish to give that proof to your rulers."

Burt ground his teeth. The thing had examined his memories? How? Then he began to feel a ghastly helplessness. For a first instant, of course, he did not distinguish between knowing his memories and knowing his thoughts. The alien's statement actually meant that he had been able to extract from Burt's braincells the recorded sensory data on which his mind had worked, but not the working of his mind on the sensory data. The thing from space did not abruptly possess himself of all Burt's knowledge. It had still to learn exactly as a baby learns, by comparing sense-perceptions with each other and abstracting ideas. But it had Burt's remembered sense-perceptions to learn from. Just as it had memories of Burt's voice to duplicate. It was duplicating Burt's voice now.

"It seems that you have done as I reasoned," said the creature without emotion. "But I cannot allow you to prove that I exist. I am in danger. You endanger me."

"You'll be damned unsafe," said Burt fiercely, "if you try to pass as a man!"

"Now, yes," it agreed. "But I know it. I have not examined all your memories."

Burt said nothing. He was staggered, but he glared. Norma held fast to his hands, breathing in a panicky tempo.

"And," said the creature from space, completely without expression, "you humans are strange. I have decided that there may well be humans in communication with my enemies, keeping their arrangement a secret from other humans, that they may profit by it. If there are such spies of my enemies among you humans, they will search for me. Here. So I must go away."

Burt did not cease to glare, but he began to hope. Norma was here. For himself, he was angrily ready to take chances. But the obligation to see Norma safely away was greater than any other obligation could possibly be.

"All right then," snapped Burt. "Go away! Nobody'd believe us if we told our story, anyhow!"

But his mind leaped ahead to what he'd be able to report to the FBI. If the scraps of plastic weren't too good as evidence, still his story and Norma's and the blunders the creature was sure to make——

"You will come with me," said the alien without emphasis. "You will be convenient for me, for a time."

Burt felt cold. But there was Norma. He clenched his hands. After all, the thing did have what it said was an atom bomb. If it had landed from space, and the drama in the sky had been its escape from its pursuers, he couldn't risk Norma's life on a guess that it bluffed about emergency weapons. Men would take emergency weapons along if they were forced to land on what to them would be a savage and a hostile world.

"I've got other plans," said Burt shortly. "What would I gain by helping you?"

If the creature needed him, he'd play hard to get. Make a bargain for knowledge; scientific information to pass on for human use.

But the alien did not answer. It was carefully examining exactly the place that Burt had just searched. for scraps of the brown plastic. It found a few morsels he'd missed. It moved to put them somewhere which was not where the pockets of Burt's clothes were. It corrected its mistake. It ignored Burt's query. He repeated it.

"I said, what would I get out of helping you?"

The so-human head turned with its utterly unhuman, unwinking regard.

"You do not understand," it said flatly. "Humans kill rats and mice because they are inconvenient. They keep dogs because they are convenient. You are intelligent. You can choose to be convenient or not. You will tell me now."

Completely without emotion, it reached inside the shirt it wore and brought out the exotically shaped metal object it had indicated was a weapon. It was convincingly without feeling one way or another.

"We will go now," it said flatly.

It did not care. Burt felt a raging humiliation because it would kill him with neither regret or elation. But he said urgently:

"You just sit here, Norma, and—don't tell anybody anything about this. They wouldn't believe you, anyhow."

The figure said as indifferently as before:

"She may be convenient. She will come also."

"No!" raged Burt. "No! You shan't——"

"I can kill her," said the alien without interest. "It does not matter."

Norma stood up. She sobbed just once. She moved very stiffly. She groped for Burt's arm and clung to it. She moved jerkily. She walked out of the house. Burt moved with her, to steady and support her. The thing followed them out. It went to the cover of the well from which the cottage water-supply was drawn. It lifted the cover with an ease which spoke of terrifying physical strength.

"For your information." it said, "you will look."

It pointed its metal object down toward the water in the well. There was a sudden flash of intolerable brightness from the weapon. The creature drew back its hand. And steam roared up out of the well in a monstrous gush that rose tree-

56

top high. It rolled and curled among the upper branches.

"Now," said the creature, "you will drive."

Burt took the wheel. He felt utterly sickened. Norma sat beside him, her face like chalk. The creature got into the back of the car.

"Drive westward," it commanded coldly. "I will stay out of sight. My face is not properly colored yet." Then it added matter-of-factly, "You understand what I will do if I am inconvenienced."

It sank down impossibly to the floor of the back of the car. Norma looked at it. Her expression became one of utter horror. Burt stared down. The body that had looked so human, looked human no longer. It had folded in upon itself. It had no bones. The flexible mask which was its face had visibly become detached from whatever was behind it. For its own idea of comfort, the fugitive from space had ceased to fill the legs of the trousers and the sleeves of the shirt. It was impossible to guess what its normal shape might be. It looked simply shapeless.

But its voice came up from the floor-boards. Burt's voice.

"Drive westward. And I shall not want attention drawn to this car."

From the mass, the mound, the blob of whatever-it-was inside the collapsed garments, the voice which was Burt's own sounded like something out of a madman's nightmare.

Burt drove away, his hands clenched tightly on the wheel. Norma sat stiffly beside him, her cheeks like marble.

Before dusk fell, Burt said in a low tone to Norma:

"We'll need some gas soon. If I were alone, I'd let the car run out of it. But—when I stop for gas, you get out and walk around. To powder your nose—anything. Try to slip away."

They were then better than a hundred miles from the lake and the place where the alien had landed. They had come partly through the mountains in whose foothills the vacation resort was located. They rode along a wide smooth highway, with some mountains against the setting sun, but western foothills visible between them.

Norma licked her lips. Four hours of driving, without a word or movement of the creature in the back of the car. Nothing had happened to reassure her, but it is not possible to sustain an acute emotion of any sort for a very long time. The hysterical horror which had cowed her as much as fear had become merely a numbed dread.

Burt showed greater signs of strain. He felt not only responsibility for Norma's safety, but that it was through him

57

that the alien was clothed and partly disguised, and might ultimately become able to conceal itself, with untoward results for all human beings. The creature might be a criminal among its own kind. It might have been pursued by interstellar avengers in the nature of police. If it were a criminal, and could hide on Earth and ultimately escape, Earth might become a galactic hideout for criminals of its stripe, ultimately to be destroyed simply to root them out. On the other hand, there might be legal warfare among the stars, and the creature might draw upon Earth the destructive weapons of a galactic civilization, or—even worse—make Earth in some sort a military base for the interstellar nation it belonged to.

But meanwhile the car hummed along the highway. Burt's throat was dry. He tried despairingly to think, but he had no material to think about. The creature knew too much. It knew all he had ever seen or done. While he was unconscious it had somehow drained his brain of all its memories, which would have been the cause of the incredible sensation of coldness inside his skull when he woke and found his thinking controlled to absorbed remembering. It would have been the creature seeking ruthlessly for a place to hide. Which it had found.

There was a highway sign, "One and one-half miles to Service Area." That would be gas-pumps and a restaurant and a shop where oil could be changed and rapairs made. Norma might be able to get into the restaurant. She might—she might!—be able to escape. But somehow he, Burt, must manage to destroy the alien or at the least disarm or disable him: in some fashion remove the danger the alien created by its mere existence alive and at liberty on Earth.

Ahead, the red sun touched the edge of the world. There was the fragrance of growing things in the breeze that blew past the car's windows.

Another sign. It said, "½ Mile to Service Area."

Burt said thickly:

"We need gas. If we are to go much further I should stop and buy more."

There were sounds in the back of the car. A shoe scraped. Something was pushed aside. Burt knew that the thing in the back was flowing from shapelessness into the legs and arms and simulacrum of a face and head that lay on the floor behind him. He could imagine it too vividly. He wanted to be sick.

Then there were stirrings. He felt a hand—he knew it would look like a hand: it was shaped like one—grasp the seat-back by his shoulder. Norma shuddered, but did not

58

look. Burt felt that the thing had raised itself and now sat human-fashion on the back seat. To a casual glance, in twilight, it would look human enough. To Burt it was perhaps more horrible for that very reason.

"I have been examining the memories I took last night," said the creature tranquilly. "You need money to pay for the gasoline. Do you have it?"

Burt nodded, fighting against the nausea his mental picture of a moment before had produced.

Burt drove on. Half a mile beyond, there was a turn-off to a filling-station with an elaborate restaurant behind it. Burt drove to a gas-pump. His voice was strained as he ordered gas. Norma did not stir. With his hand held so that it was not visible from the back, he gestured urgently for her to get out of the car—of course assuming that she would make some excuse.

She sat still, trembling. Once he saw her move as if to try to rise, but it was as if her legs would not support her.

The pump-bell clanged and clanged. Then the tank was full. Burt paid. The attendant wiped off the windshield. Burt drove out of the service area and back on the highway.

A long time after—when it was dark—Burt said desperately:

"Have you decided where you want me to drive you?"

Somehow it had not been possible to question the creature while it lay withdrawn into shapelessness on the floor of the car. When it had human form, horrible as it was, it was at least possible to address it.

His own voice came back to him.

"I have made plans." Then, suddenly, the voice ceased to be toneless. "Your memories, on careful examination, tell me that I have not fully spoken your language. There are not only words, but tones. From now on, I shall vary this voice as you do. I shall practice. You will listen and tell me when I do not speak quite like a human being."

Burt swallowed, dry-throated.

"Now I shall speak pleasantly," said the voice. And it did. Its intonation became cordial: "I realize now how Norma knew I was not a man. The teeth of my face are not bright. From your memories I think the inside of the mouth should have a different look. The skin that shows should look differently. And your memories say that there is make-up to change the look of the skin, and it can be bought in drug-stores. You will find a town. I wish you to buy the make-up that will make this face look quite human."

The tone, by its inappropriate cordiality, made the whole

59

speech a grisly performance. And there was an odd uncertainty in the use of words substituted for color.

Burt drove on. The sky overhead grew darker. Stars appeared. There were shadows in the underbrush and woods beside the road. They turned slowly black. Burt saw Norma moving on the seat beside him. Suddenly she gave a little cry.

"What's the matter?" he demanded.

"I—I can move again!" she gasped. "At the filling station I couldn't!"

The now-pleasant voice from the back of the car said:

"I used a very small power-charge so that she could not rise. It has worn off now. I did not want her to run away. It would have been inconvenient for me to have to destroy the filling-station and restaurant. My pursuers might learn of it if they have spies among you humans."

Burt drove and drove and drove. Other cars showed headlights, some bright and some dim. Burt's mind had practically ceased to work rationally. He had considered violating traffic laws so that a motorcycle policeman would stop him. But the alien's weapon—judged by the flash of fire down the well —was deadly. To attract attention of the police would mean simply the death of a policeman. He had thought of crashing head-on into another car or running it over a cliff or through the guard-rail of a bridge. He would have been willing to get himself killed, in such a desperate measure, but there was Norma. His ability to think was exhausted. He couldn't work out anything more.

Cars, coming from the opposite direction, made occasional rushing sounds as they flowed long the road toward Burt, and then boomed gustily past. The highway curved through longer, easier curvings as the foothills grew less. It rolled up and down grades that were less and less noticeable.

Half an hour after leaving the filling-station, there were twinklings of light yet miles away against the dark horizon.

"There's a town ahead," said Burt, wearily. He wasn't afraid, now. The sensation of fear was worn out. "You want me to stop at a drug-store."

The voice behind him said cordially:

"I will sit in the car. With Norma. But first stop the car beside the road at some convenient place."

"What——?"

"I wish to demonstrate something," said the voice. "So you will understand why you must do as I say. I shall not hurt either of you."

Burt felt shame. It was deep humiliation to be commanded by a creature which was not even human. He had not the sick hatred that would have come of knowing he was afraid. He wasn't. He knew that he was capable of doing anything, up to and including getting himself killed, if only it dealt fully with the fugitive from space. All the pride that humans take for granted in their superiority to all other living things, was outraged by this being's attitude. It regarded humans as vermin, like rats or mice. It would make use of them as humans made use of dogs. And to Burt it had become much less important to stay alive than to justify his humanity.

He turned off the concrete onto the road's turfed shoulder. The highway ran through a deep cut, here. He stopped the car. The motor idled. There was the sound of night-things, and stars shone overhead, and somewhere a nightbird called. There was the feel of life all about. The grass and trees and even the cut-away stone of the hillside seemed alive and familiar. But the thing in the back—that was purest, hackle-raising, hateable alienness. A frightening thing.

It stirred, on the rear seat. With uncanny deftness it cranked down the window on the side next the road.

"I told you," it said cordially, "that I had an emergency weapon. Your race has not yet begun to understand atomic energy. And you, Burt, have been thinking of ways to destroy me. So I show you my weapon. It releases energy under close control, from so little that Norma did not feel the beam that paralyzed her, to all the energy of its fuel-store at one instant. And it is much more efficient than your uranium bombs, Burt."

Burt waited dully. He was not really aware of any emotion except exhaustion and a hatred that was so deep-rooted that it was as much a part of him as his name. It was pure, primeval instinct to hate anything which dared to put itself on equality with man. And this creature set itself above!

The headlights shone on the rocky side-wall of the cut. The road curved on ahead. There were the multitudinous sounds of the night. The creature said placidly:

"My speaking should be more human now. Is it?"

Burt said harshly: "Yes."

He waited. Nothing happened. Only the night-noises and the night-smells, and the sound of the idling motor. But there came a grumbling sound. It was a motor-truck, approaching around the curve and climbing a hill.

The truck's headlights came around the curve. It was a

huge, aluminum-painted oil-truck. There were huge, red, black-bordered letters on its side, spelling out GASOLINE. It reached the top of the grade, and Burt heard its gears shift, and it came on. It went past on the other side of the highway, rumbling and clanking and roaring as such trucks do.

The thing in the back moved its arm, clad in the sleeve of Burt's shirt. A metal object glinted. There was a flash of unbearably brilliant light.

The gasoline-truck burst into flame from one end to the other. Its tank body shattered. A flood of flaming liquid spouted skyward and went racing over the highway and splashed against the walls of the cut. There was a lake of leaping flames which made the highway and its rocky sidewalls brighter than day.

And the truck rolled onward. Fallen flaming gasoline drenched its cab and hood and burned man-height high before it. Running burning gasoline flowed along beside it.

It rolled and rolled and rolled, sending thirty-foot flames skyward, moving in the middle of an inferno. The highway straightened. The truck continued to curve. It ran off the concrete and into a ditch and stopped there, burning.

Burt had the door of the car open to rush to the aid of the driver. He could not hope to do anything, but the action was automatic.

"The driver is dead," said his own voice from the back of the car. "The energy killed him as it blasted the truck. Get back in the car."

Burt plunged toward the flames.

His arms and legs—his whole body—became as water. He felt himself tumbling to the concrete. Norma cried out. Burt lay on the road. He had no feeling in any of his members. He could only see and hear.

The voice said placidly:

"Get back in the car."

The power of motion returned to Burt's limbs and body. He panted incoherently at the thing from space, his fists clenched as he staggered upright. The voice said tonelessly:

"I will be inconvenienced if I need to throw you in the flames. Get in the car."

Norma cried out pleadingly. And Burt came out of a moment of fury so horrible as to be unrememberable. The truck burned terribly, but there was no outcry from inside it. There had been no one. If the driver had been alive, at the least there would have been screams.

Burt gasped and choked and panted almost unintelligibly:

"I'll kill you for this! I'll kill you! I'll kill——"

"Get in the car!" cried Norma shrilly. "Please! For my sake!"

And the idea of Norma alone with the creature and purest horror was the one thing that could move Burt just then. He stumbled toward the car. He did not want to. He would have preferred to be killed. But there was Norma, and there was the other fact that if he were killed nobody but Norma would know that the creature from space did exist and was on Earth.

He slid under the wheel, drunk with hatred.

"Drive on, now," said the alien.

Burt drove on, his hands shaking and tightening convulsively.

The creature in the back said calmly:

"I have studied your memories. I think you plan to disobey me. Whenever I think you plan to disobey me I shall kill a human. You will blame yourself. You will be right. If you do disobey me I will kill you and all other humans nearby."

Burt's teeth clamped together as he drove. He was half-blind with rage. Beside him, Norma trembled. The car went on and on and on. They passed a car coming from the direction in which they were headed. It would encounter the still-burning tank-truck. A little later, they passed an interurban bus, bound the same way. A fierce hope sprang up in Burt that when the truck was discovered——But there had been no missile. A blast of pure heat—pure energy—had exploded and ignited the truck's cargo. Examination of the burned-out shell would tell nothing to men who did not even suspect that a weapon like the alien's could exist.

There was simply no answer to the situation.

Miles later—and here the land was nearly flat—the lights of the town glittered very near. Here the traffic was heavier. There were many cars on the highway. As the town drew nearer and nearer, highway-speed could no longer be maintained. Burt found himself trailing another car. Its brake-lights flashed on. Burt slowed sharply.

A fast truck came roaring out of the town. It had the regulation headlights, and extra bright red warning-lights which flicked on and off beside them. Traffic bunched and pulled aside to give it right of way. It went rushing past the red warning-lights securing it right of way. Its noise diminished toward the highway cut in which the truck had exploded. It had been discovered—still burning—and help telephoned for.

63

The traffic near the town resumed its normal speed, once the rescue-truck had gone on its way.

His voice came from the creature in the back.

"I do not identify that truck from your memories," said the voice. "Why did the other cars make way for it?"

Burt had not seen red warning-lights used in exactly that arrangement before, but of course he knew its purpose.

"It's a rescue truck," he said, hating. "It's going to try to help the poor devil you killed back yonder. They'll be too late, but they'll try."

There was a pause. Burt's features were drawn and savage. The alien said reflectively:

"It is not in your memories. How did you know?"

"The blinking lights," snapped Burt. "They were red. It couldn't be anything else."

"Red," said the thing in the back. "That is what you call a color. Colors are important to you humans?"

"To us humans, yes," said Burt harshly.

Silence again. The town was very near. Houses appeared on either side of the highway. Street-lights. The alien pressed itself into the darkest corner.

"Here you will buy the colors for my face and skin," it said tonelessly once more.

"I will buy it," agreed Burt in the very quintessence of quiet hate. "I will not give you an excuse to kill anybody else. There's a drug-store ahead. I'm going to buy grease-paint and lipstick and powder. I have money to pay for it."

The creature said: "I know. Your memories have told me of the need for money, now that I am on your world. First I need to make this face look just right."

The car was actually in the town by this time. For two or three blocks there was a narrow street with residences rising abruptly from the sidewalk-line. The traffic here ran bumper-to-bumper. Sidestreets were wider, and Burt could tell that many were tree-lined, with branches meeting above the pavement. The air was full of the smell of engine-exhausts. Ahead, traffic-lights glinted red and green and there was a brightness which would be the business section of whatever town this might be. There would certainly be a drug-store here.

The way widened at the first traffic light, and here was the most miniature of great White Ways—a movie theater with a brilliantly lighted marquee, an hotel with a sign; stores, confectionery -open—a bakery. There was a drug-store on a street corner.

Burt turned off the main street and stopped and parked just beyond the turn. He could look into the side windows of the drug-store and see the customers. Two giggling teen-age girls, consuming sodas. A fat woman, without a hat, waiting for a prescription. Behind the car, on the main street, was an unending sound of traffic.

Burt got out of the car and went into the drug-store. The commonplaceness, the complete normality of the scene and the people around him, was so strange as to be shocking. Here were the smells of ice-cream flavoring and perfume and antiseptics and newsprint from the magazine-stand, all blended together into a perfectly typical well-known odor. These people were thinking about everyday things—where they had come from, where they'd go next, what so-and-so had said—without any doubt about the permanence of all familiar things.

But outside, in the car, there was a creature who regarded all human beings as vermin. Burt had a sense of unreality, of an insistent disbelief in the reality of things. This small town was reality. Enormous emptinesses between stars, and strange worlds from which ships made voyages, and creatures with not even permanent shapes of their own—they were preposterous!

But when the druggist came to wait on him, Burt heard himself asking for grease-paint and lipstick and powder and eyebrow pencil and a mirror. For what amounted to a make-up kit to cause a plastic mask to look human.

As he picked his wares, the druggist offered a lipstick with a red faked jewel in its top. The faceted glass glittered redly. And suddenly Burt realized an overwhelmingly important fact of which he hadn't been aware before. It was that the alien absolutely, positively, certainly could never hope to pass for a human being among humans without the help of some human being that it trusted! Any captive it might secure could always make the alien betray itself! Not one could ever fail to learn of his power to unmask the thing from emptiness! The alien had to have human friends to survive. Friends!

Because it was color-blind.

It knew that colors existed. It had somehow absorbed all of Burt's sensory memories. But it could not perceive colors, itself. It had not been able to tell that the flashing lights on the rescue-truck were red ones. It had asked if colors were important.

It could not possibly learn to use make-up so that the job would deceive a human eye, because its eyes were different

65

from human ones! And very probably it could not even grasp the significance of variations in tints it could not perceive!

Burt paid for the make-up and went out to the car again. Norma was sobbing quietly to herself. She gasped in relief when Burt came back. She clutched his arm and held on to it.

"I was so—frightened!" she gasped. "If I'm ever left alone with it again, I'll die!"

Burt started the motor. He said grimly, over his shoulder:

"I've got the make-up for your mask and hands. Where shall I drive you now?"

He saw the bronze-colored face in the rear-view mirror. Its eyes were fixed upon him.

"Drive to some secluded place," said the alien placidly, "where I can make myself convincingly human. Then I will tell you of an enterprise to get the money you use and that I need. I will need a great deal."

Burt drove. Around the block, and when a green light showed he got back into the stream of through traffic. There was no conversation. There were only the sounds of the traffic and once a sudden blaring of music which was probably a car radio in passing.

The last traffic-light. Beyond it, speeds rose. The cars drew apart. The highway went out of town, and presently bored through farmland and woodland and once past a marshy meadow in which frogs croaked resonantly to the stars. They came upon occasional side-roads. Most of them obviously led to farmhouses, but presently Burt braked abruptly. There was a cart-track, unpaved and barely marked by wheels, which led into a second-growth pine-thicket. Burt inspected it in the bright yellow light of the headlights.

"This looks like a suitable make-up room," he said grimly. "A little way in, you should be invisible. You'd use the dome light for your artwork."

"You may drive in," said the voice behind him.

Burt entered in low gear. Weeds grew in the middle. Three-inch and four-inch and five-inch saplings crowded close to the track on either hand. The abandoned road turned this way and that. Two hundred yards in, Burt stopped and switched off the headlights. He turned off the motor. The musical sounds of a summer night came in the car's open windows. The traffic on the highway was still audible, but not even a glint of headlights came through the trees.

Burt switched on the light inside the car and presented his purchases to the bronze-colored figure in the rear seat, which looked so much like a human being—and was so horrible because it did not look entirely like one.

"You know how to use this," said Burt curtly, "if you do know everything I ever did. I did some amateur theatricals in college."

The alien nodded benignly. Its flexible plastic fingers deftly opened the wrapped parcel Burt handed over.

"Your memories," it said blandly, "are excellent preparation for passing as a human on this world."

It spread out the make-up kit. It set up the mirror. It began to work with the grease-paint, smearing the flesh-colored stuff over its brown plastic skin. Burt watched. Then he spoke to it in a low voice.

"I think I should tell you," he said quietly, "that you are color-blind."

The figure regarded itself in the mirror.

"When you think," said Burt, "you'll realize that it's important. You're color-blind! You can't pass as a human without the help of human beings you can trust. Trust, remember! The only way you can live safely and securely on this world is to make a proper bargain with our government. You'll be given an asylum and concealment in exchange for technical information."

The thing said coldly:

"Are you thinking to deceive me?"

"No," said Burt. "To enlighten you."

The creature ignored him. It worked the grease-paint into the plastic. Its face and throat and neck. Its cunningly formed hands and arms up to what should have been its elbows. It seemed able to recall every movement Burt had made, years before, making up for collegiate amateur theatricals.

It was infernally intelligent. It had infernally great abilities. Between a little after last midnight and the time of Burt's awakening near noon of today, it had learned to speak English by the examination of his memories. In the same time it had made for itself, out of the plastic of its parachute, a flexible human body, very near to perfection among things of the kind. These were strictly individual achievements, not depending solely on the technology its race had developed. And these were evidences of a kind of intelligence that Burt would have admired—however reluctantly in an alien—but for the wholly unreasonable fact that the creature did not normally have a human-shaped body.

As he watched, Burt saw it make astonishingly human-like

motions. But suddenly it did something which shocked him out of all reason, for the thing that it was. The alien had used its humanoid form with skill, bending the arms only at the shoulder and elbow and wrist. But it did not actually have bones. It found some clumsiness in its pretense of humanity. It bent its left forearm to reach something, exactly as if there had been a fourth joint there, or else as if there had been bones and both had snapped. And Burt's stomach protested violently at the sight.

The thing looked in the mirror. It applied lipstick. It put the stuff horribly into the mouth of its mask, working it about. It applied tooth-enamel to its brown teeth. It looked estimatingly at Burt—turning whiter and sicker as the process went on—for a comparison.

Norma grew more and more tense as the travesty of humanity developed, according to the alien's own best perception of what would be perfectly deceptive to the eye.

"In a little while," said the creature tonelessly, "you will drive me back into the town we just left. Your memories tell me that for money you creatures will do anything. Money will buy anything. I will get money. Your memories even tell me where to get it and what the safe of a bank is like. My energy weapon, of course, will make it easy."

Burt stared, his eyes wide in astounded unbelief.

"You mean." he said in flat incredulity, "that you—with the knowledge you've got—the technology you know about —the civilization you represent—you'll come to Earth and rob a bank?"

The alien said flatly:

"Of course. It will be convenient to have money. Naturally I will take it. You are only human beings."

Norma had neither eaten nor drunk since morning, nor Burt for a longer time than that, but neither of them thought of such things now. The creature from space completed its make-up job to its own satisfaction. Then it said tonelessly:

"Now you will take me to the bank."

"It will be unwise now," said Burt. He added bitterly, "I'm not thinking of your welfare! But with a lot of people about the streets, there is more likely to be an alarm. If you're interrupted, you may have to kill a hundred people to get away."

The alien spoke without emotion. "You would kill a hundred mice."

"The point is." Burt told it doggedly, "that human bank-robbers can't kill a hundred people! If you do, it will be evi-

68

dent that you aren't human. If it becomes evident that a bank has been robbed by a non-human creature, the newspapers will be full of it. The radio news will broadcast it. If your enemies have agents on earth, they'll know it immediately."

The eyes in the grease-painted mask regarded him unwaveringly. Burt knew that a search was being made among the memories that had been stolen from him, for sensory data to confirm or refute what he had just said. The alien knew sounds Burt had heard, but it had had to work out for itself what words might mean. It knew newspaper headlines Burt had read, but it had to deduce from words spoken about them, what the newspapers said. It had had less than twenty-four hours in which to acquire—by second-hand experience—a knowledge of a human world. It had done, so far, better than any human being could possibly do. But there were bound to be limits to its ability to understand, so soon.

It said, after a moment:

"Yes. Your memories justify what you have said. I shall wait until humans sleep."

It sat quietly in the back. After a moment it said:

"Turn out the light."

Burt turned out the light. There was silence. Above the cart-track there was a narrow band of stars. Frogs croaked somewhere a little way off. Burt felt a slight movement beside him. He reached out and Norma's hand closed frightenedly over his. There was not much reassurance he could give her.

"I should repeat to you," said Burt steadily to the darkness behind him, "that you need human help. You are color-blind!"

"You will explain," said the voice in the back.

"Your eyes do not see as ours do. There is color. The word does not mean anything to you. Maybe you see by what to us is in infra-red. But you do not see as we do. You cannot make up your face, by your eyesight, to look right by ours."

"My face and hands are like yours now," said the alien. "I compared. I know."

"You can't tell!" insisted Burt doggedly. "You do not look like a human. You look like a zombie! If you speak to a woman, she will scream. Speak to a man, and he will be frightened! You look like hell—to us!"

The alien said coldly:

"Turn on the light."

Burt turned on the light. The alien said:

69

"Norma. Turn and look at me."

Slowly, the girl turned. The creature in the back should have looked like a man. But it had used powder and its skin was a sickly dead white. It had shadowed under its eyes, because there were shadows under Burt's eyes now. Its own unwinking orbs were enormously emphasized, so that they looked terrifyingly remote from humankind—as they were. Its mouth was vividly red, and wrongly shaped.

Norma gasped.

She looked as if in another instant she would cry out shrilly.

"Turn out the light," said the alien.

Burt turned out the light. He could not tell if the alien were offended in its vanity—or if it had vanity. He could not tell whether its intelligence was so great that it would recognize facts which its intellect must discern, but which its senses could not verify, or whether it had a pride-of-race equal to the impassioned pride of men, so that it could not admit itself to be dependent on inferior creatures.

"I shall test this," said the alien tonelessly. "I shall see how other humans act when they see me. If you have lied I shall kill you both."

Burt licked his lips. He said steadily:

"There is nothing on earth I want to do more than to kill you. But I tell the truth. You cannot live on Earth without men. You cannot force men to serve you. I can arrange for my government to bargain with you—even forgive the murder of that poor devil in the tank-truck because you didn't know what you were doing. I offer to get you a hiding-place and protection from your enemies and secrecy so your existence won't be known to them. But you'll have to trade the technical information you have and that we haven't got yet. Unless you make that bargain—you're finished! And you can take it or leave it!"

It was an ultimatum which was absolutely based on fact. But it was not one that a man could take from a lower animal. It was not one that the alien could take from men.

Burt's muscles abruptly seemed to turn to water. He slumped in his seat. Norma, simultaneously, went absolutely limp. The two of them sagged helplessly where they sat. They were conscious, but unable to move. They were two utterly inert heaps on the front-seat cushion. They could not even try to stir. Burt, at first, could only hate helplessly.

Nothing happened. Nothing. The alien had reduced the two to helplessness as a man might tether a horse. It did

70

not want to pay attention to them. It numbed them to wait for it to use them again.

The helplessness lasted for a very long time indeed. The night-insects chirruped and stridulated outside the car. The breeze blew softly among the pine branches. The thing from space remained perfectly still. It waited for an appropriate time to leave this place and go back to the town through which it had recently passed. Perhaps it meditated upon materials to be bought, machines to be contrived, devices to be duplicated, and ultimately a headlong rush through space away from this world. For such purposes, money would be required, humans would have to be bribed, workshops established. The alien prepared to secure money as the practical means of getting things done on the planet Earth. It was the most practical way. So the creature from the stars would use the technology of a race that had conquered interstellar space, and the powers developed in a thousand thousand years of progress—to rob a bank in a small country town.

It seemed centuries, but it was really no more than two hours before feeling and strength returned together in a rush to Burt's arms and legs and body. In those two hours, Burt had had perforce to think. He had thought with some clarity, if not to any encouraging purpose. But because he no longer had any illusions about the entity in the back seat of his car, he could never feel any more fear of it. Even his fears for Norma were changed in kind. He no longer hated the alien to any great degree. But he knew, now, a deep and implacable enmity for the creature that did not need hatred for energy. The alien was an enemy of mankind because of its very constitution. Because it existed. Because it was what it was. It might be a criminal among its own kind, or it might be in some unimaginable fashion a very gallant soldier. But on Earth it was an outlaw and foe.

Burt raised himself carefully and helped Norma again to sit upright. The thing said:

"You will drive me to the town. I intend to rob the bank. Then I will have money to hire men to serve me. You are not as useful as you could be."

There might have been a sneer in the last phrase, but Burt could not tell. He said in a voice as completely without emotion as the creature's own:

"I will need to turn the car around."

He started the motor. He turned on the headlights. He looked at Norma, shuddering in the seat beside him.

"All right, Norma?"

She moistened her lips and nodded, breathing fast.

He turned the car a hundred yards on, in a weed-grown open field. He drove back through the thicket. Presently he came out on the highway, and the traffic was much thinner now, and he crossed the road and headed back the way he had come.

It had been nearer three hours than two since he stopped at the drug-store for make-up. The drug-store was closed. In the brightly lighted four-block business section there was practically no traffic at all. The marquee of the movie theater was dark. There was a car parked at a filling-station, getting gas before that station closed too. There was only one pedestrian on the sidewalk, and he turned a corner and vanished as Burt drove past the first traffic light. That light made small clicking sounds and turned red. After a decorous interval, it made other clicking sounds and turned green again.

Burt drove with great calmness to a position opposite the bank. He drew in to the curb and stopped.

"There are still cars coming through here," he said coldly, "so if you break in the front door it will be noticed and you will be interrupted. To keep you from killing people, I suggest that you break in from the back. There will undoubtedly be a burglar-alarm, which I do not doubt you will set off."

The creature said tonelessly:

"You will wait here."

It opened the rear car-door and walked across the street. Burt said calmly:

"I can't move my legs. Can you, Norma?"

"N-no," said Norma very quietly. "We'll have to wait."

Burt turned his head and watched the alien in motion. It looked convincingly human at any one moment, but the sum of several moments was less than satisfying. But it happened that no car passed through the town at just this moment. The creature's face had not been seen by anybody but Burt and Norma, up to this time.

Burt watched with an odd detachment. He had stopped feeling anything in particular except a strong conviction that sooner or later the alien would slip in some fashion and he would kill it—or someone would. It was not at all a usual way to feel. Burt did not analyze his sensations, but if an opportunity had arisen to cause the alien's death at the cost of his own, he would have seized it with the most matter-of-fact promptness. The thing, indeed, intended to kill him presently because he was not a good nor satisfactory domestic animal.

The thing from space, wearing Burt's clothes, walked into an alleyway beside the bank. Its gait was near but not quite the way a man walks. It undulated. It vanished.

"It's going to kill us, I think," said Norma quietly.

"I think that's the intention," agreed Burt. "I'm sorry, Norma. You can't walk, can you? I can't."

She shook her head. She said steadily:

"I don't think we matter. If you can crash the car somehow, Burt, so it'll be sure to be killed . . ."

He nodded, and said with a warmth that was peculiar, under the circumstances:

"You're a good sport. I'm sorry you're in this, but you're a good partner for anything. Even dying, if it comes to that."

There was a very small noise across the street. Something like cracklings. Then a thump.

"He's getting in a door," said Burt. "He'd burn it in. I would guess he set off a burglar-alarm, but I don't hear anything. Maybe there'll be police—poor devils!"

"You can't drive?"

"Not without feet to use," he told her. "The starter's on the floor, and the accelerator too. I'm afraid not."

They waited. Burt's mind no longer hunted frantically for ways to escape the creature now in the bank. He only searched continually and coldly for a way to thwart or destroy it. The emergency weapon was the key to everything. It had to be gotten rid of. Even if the creature were killed, and Burt with it, that weapon had to be disposed of so it could not possibly be picked up by somebody and set off by accident or deliberately out of curiosity.

"It's odd," said Norma absorbedly, "how one gets past being afraid. You aren't, Burt. I like you for it."

He said deliberately:

"If we'd lived, I think we'd have married. I hope so. I like you too."

They looked at each other. It seemed almost humorous to have taken time out for a mutual avowal of sentiment while waiting outside a bank that was being robbed, for the creature who abstractedly intended to kill them. Norma smiled faintly.

A curious small scratching noise came from the bank-building across the street. The front of the building was unchanged of course. But around the edges of a window with

73

a drawn-down shade, a flickering blue-white glow appeared. It had the uncertain waverings of electric sparks: of a torch: an arc.

"It's burning into the safe," said Burt. "It will pass for a thermit job, maybe. That weapon is versatile! Paralysis-gun, heat-ray, electric arc—and it says it can be detonated as a bomb."

The nearest traffic light clicked and changed color. A red convertible roared in low gear. It hurtled down the empty street and was gone. The light at the edge of the bank-building window attracted no attention. The noise was very faint indeed. Maybe the arc which made it would create interference in radio or television sets, but the hour was late.

"Queer we're so calm," said Norma. "I haven't a bit of hope, but I don't feel hysterical. The creature will be killed sooner or later, of course."

"It's too bad we can't read its memories as it read mine," said Burt wrily. "If there are ships among the stars—and there are—it could tell us how they're made. And that weapon is no bigger than a revolver. If our scientists could only work on that . . ."

There was a muffled thud across the street. It was not loud enough to attract attention. The two in the car were especially conscious of it, of course. They were quite helpless, with the lower part of their bodies paralyzed by the exotic alien emergency device. They could not hope to attract the attention of other humans. There was nobody else on the street. If they called anybody, the alien would hear. If they managed to get themselves lifted out of the car, or if they signalled another car to a stop, the alien would kill other humans— kill in wholesale lots—to destroy them. There was no purpose to be served by getting other people killed with nothing else achieved.

The traffic lights clicked and changed color. There was no car waiting to take advantage of a green light. There was tranquility. Street-lamps on brick pavements, closed-up stores. In one darkened window a ring-shaped light around one special advertising sign blinked senselessly off and on. There was the smell of tree-shaded streets in the air. The traffic lights clicked and changed.

The alien walked out of the lane beside the bank. It carried a bag. It crossed the sidewalk and strode across the street to the car. At a distance it looked human, but nearby the make-up on its face was unearthly. The face was white like the belly of a dead fish. It had put deep blue shadows under its eyes. They were staring, unwinking eyes at best. They looked demoniac in the dead-white face.

It opened the back of the car and put the bag inside.

"There is a great deal of coin," the voice said tonelessly. "You will come and carry part of it."

It stood by the partly opened back door. Its plastic hand disappeared. Life and feeling and strength came back to the lower part of Burt's body. He could move his legs again.

The traffic light clicked and changed color. Down the street, behind Burt, a car-motor roared. The thing from space turned.

Burt was in the act of unfastening the door beside him when the unseen car behind—going the same way Burt's car was headed—whined shrilly as it accelerated. Burt was stepping down into the street when the speeding car's horn blatted fiercely. The unknown driver was acting as some people do. The instant the traffic-light changed, he had shot his car ahead, shifted gear, and jammed down the accelerator to streak through the lighted empty street at sixty miles an hour.

When the horn blatted the alien turned sharply. And maybe under any other circumstances the driver could have swerved in time. But the alien turned upon him the face of a walking corpse, a zombie, something with glittering eyes straight out of hell itself. A metal object appeared in its hands.

The car hit. There was an indescribably horrible thud. But even more horrible was the way the alien's body yielded to the impact. It did not crush, as the body of a man with bones would have done. It flexed. It bent. It *flowed* into a cup-like, completely impossible flattened mass—still clothed in Burt's garments—which clung to the front of the speeding car for twenty feet or more and then dropped slackly in the highway. And the car raced on ahead.

Burt glimpsed the driver's face for the fraction of an instant. It was a mask of unbelieving horror. The car roared desperately into the distance. The driver did not look back.

Then Burt realized two things simultaneously. One was that the metal object—the alien's weapon—had been knocked from its grasp. It had skidded to a stop no more than ten feet from where Burt stood absurdly with one foot on the pavement. The other was the fact that the mass of clothing which lay in the highway a little distance off, no longer looked even remotely human.

The arms and legs were empty. The head was deflated. The face had collapsed like an empty flexible mask—which it was

75

—and lay at an impossible angle to its neck. And the trunk of the body was no longer the rough flattened-cylinder shape which is proper to a human body. This thing bulged. It was almost a globe. It changed and was almost egg-shaped. It writhed and pulsated like a monstrous ameboid thing inside its human garmenture.

The sight of it was pure horror, in the deserted, brightly lighted street of a small town on a summer night. The thing inside the garments writhed blindly, and extended pseudo-pods within the enclosing cloth, and the empty, collapsed face and head turned foolishly, and the flattened, empty arms and legs jerked and stirred without purpose . . .

Burt picked up the metal thing which was the weapon the creature had used for everything from the demonstration-murder of an oil-truck driver to the burning open of a small bank's safe. He was icy cold, and he had thought he could have no further emotional reactions, but his stomach turned at the sight of the movements of the thing in the street.

He put the weapon in his pocket. He started the car. He drove savagely away. By instinct he swerved to avoid hitting the writhing thing. It was not that he meant to spare it. In taking its weapon, he had destroyed it. But he felt an over-whelming revulsion to touching it with anything—even the wheels of his car.

He roared away. But he could not help glancing behind in the rear-view mirror. The last glimpse he had of it showed it resuming human shape. When it was a bare speck in the mirror it was upraised on four stumpy projections, but the head-mask dangled emptily. It might be beginning to reform arms and legs.

Burt jammed down the accelerator. He wanted to get away from there! Beside him, above the whistling of wind past the car's windows, he heard Norma's teeth chattering.

Simply not having the alien in the car was enough to pro-duce a completely fictitious feeling of safety. It was an enor-mous relief merely not to be near the monster any longer. True, Norma's legs—as she told Burt—had no sensation in them. She and Burt had both been left helpless while the alien opened the bank safe. Burt had been released from helplessness to carry loot. But Norma was still incapacitated.

"It'll be a hospital for you," said Burt grimly. "But the first need is to get as far away as possible from where we've marooned the thing. It hasn't got its weapon now. It has to hide. But it's infernally intelligent and it could be deadly even unarmed. So we want to get away!"

Norma said quickly: "We shouldn't try to use the—weapon to free me. It could, but we don't know how to use it."

Burt nodded. They were half an hour away from the place of their escape. The road was straight and empty before them. They were back in the foothills, and trees and hillsides flashed into view in the headlight rays and swept swiftly toward them, and then darted past and were gone.

Burt brought out the weapon he'd picked up. He looked at it in the light of the instrument-board. It was completely cryptic. There was no handle designed for a human hand to grasp —though the creature had been able to use its plastic human-seeming hands to hold and use it. It was flat and irregular in shape, and there were studs on both sides. They were recessed, and it was obviously from pressure upon different combinations of them that the instrument acted in different fashions—as a paralysis-beam or a heat-ray or—so the creature had said—could detonate as an atomic bomb. It would not be possible to guess in advance which studs would release Norma from her helplessness.

Burt put it away.

"When I get a chance I'm going to fix it so it can't be turned on accidentally."

He felt perfectly safe, but he had overlooked something. A human criminal parachuted among savages would be cock-of-the-walk only so long as he had modern weapons. If he were disarmed, he would need to hide. Burt inevitably thought of the alien as like a civilized man among primitives. He hadn't seen it, actually, except clothed and masked as a man. But the creature did not think of itself as a civilized man among savages. It had phrased its viewpoint with precision when it likened its view of men to Burt's view of rats and mice. Its attitude toward mankind was that of a man to rats.

An armed human among intelligent rats would be at ease. Disarmed, he would be less at ease. But he would not hide. He would try instantly and furiously to recover his weapons or make new ones.

The alien would not try to hide because he was disarmed.

But Burt didn't happen to reason in that obvious fashion. He meant to drive the night through and get completely out of the area in which the thing must—he considered—conceal itself. He had evidence to demand instant belief and cooperation from the FBI. He had loot from a bank, and when the manner of its robbery was examined carefully, it would check with Burt's tale. The alien would have burned open a door, where a human would get in more easily. Even the burned-open safe would not appear a torch job when carefully looked over. There was the fact of the burned oil-truck. There was Norma's present condition. Above all, X-ray examination of the alien weapon would prove its non-human origin. A quiet and grim hunt would instantly be made for the fugitive from space. It would be captured. Then the bargain Burt had offered would be forced upon it. It would tell whatever it knew that could be useful to humans. Or else.

Then Norma said shakily:

"I think my legs are coming to life again!"

Burt was not a particularly safe driver, for a while. He was desperately intent upon the symptoms of Norma's recovery from the paralysis-beam. He did not even notice when the car roared through a deep cut, past a place where the road's surface was seared with fire, and the rocky side-walls were sooted, and the grass and weeds off the concrete were burned to gray ash. But the remains of the oil-truck had been taken away.

They went on and on through the night, and Norma found sensation returning, and the power of movement, and presently she said exultantly that she could walk and wanted to try.

Under the circumstances, a certain lack of forethought was natural.

They stopped at the very first of the service areas which by its lights was open for business at this hour. Burt had the gas-tank filled at the pump. Norma got out and walked about, exuberantly.

"It's wonderful!" she said softly, stopping by Burt's side of the car. "I feel giddy! I feel light-headed." Then she smiled at him. "And—I think we know each other now, Burt, after what we've been through. I like what I know about you."

"We'll get something to eat," said Burt, "and then go on. Nothing much can be done before morning, anyhow."

He drove over to the diner, but Norma walked for joy in the obedience of her legs to her will. They were smiling at each other when they entered the diner which here catered to the public.

Burt always remembered that moment. There was a counter, and stools before it, and a stout man reading a newspaper. He had a radio turned on. As Burt and Norma walked in, he jerked his head to stare at the instrument.

"—*apparently a maniac*," said a reedy voice, "*walked up to the filling-station attendant and attacked him without warning. He broke his neck, then approached the car, whose*

78

driver threatened him with a revolver. The maniac seized the arm holding the pistol and with super-human strength pulled the driver out through the window. He dashed him to the ground, killing him instantly. He then climbed in the car, but the driver's wife, in the back, opened the door and jumped out, screaming. The maniac headed east on the post highway, the car swerving crazily. The only living witness, the woman whose husband was killed, hysterically insists that the maniac has a dead-white face and glittering eyes. It is presumed that now he is armed . . ."

Burt took Norma's arm and turned her around. They walked out of the diner again. Both of them were ashen-white. Burt led the way fiercely to the car. They were almost at it when a car came racing furiously along the way they had come. It swerved and roared into the service area. Burt put his hand on Norma's shoulder and pressed her fiercely downward.

"Behind the car!" he commanded thickly. "It's here!"

He watched through the car's windows from the outside. The other car braked to a stop, with screamings of tortured brake-bands. A figure got out of it. It went toward the diner. It passed within twenty feet of Burt and Norma, but the car was between. It went into the diner.

It was the alien.

Burt thrust Norma into the car and closed the door with a desperate softness. He plunged to the alien's car and snatched out its ignition key.

There were sounds inside the diner. The fat man, inside there, had turned from a broadcast about a maniac with a white face and eyes like a ghoul. He looked up to see what looked like a zombie with a white face and eyes like a fiend from hell. The creature asked a question in an unhuman, toneless voice. The fat man gagged and goggled. He made absurd pawing motions in the air, as if to push the alien away. When the alien moved toward him, the fat man screamed.

Burt was in the act of letting in the clutch when he heard the shots. He was in the act of darting out the service-area exit to the highway again, when the alien came out of the diner. It had heard the retreating car. It began to run, very terribly, in pursuit. But it could not overtake the roaring car in all-out flight.

It was a long time later and many miles along the road before Burt could steady his voice to speak. Then he said in horror-struck revulsion:

79

"It was—coming after us! For its weapon! I got the ignition-key of its car . . ."

He nursed his car around a curve engineered for forty miles an hour. He was doing better than seventy. The road became a straightaway and the speedometer needle climbed higher, higher, and higher yet.

Norma said faintly: "The filling-station man—"

"I think," said Burt grimly, "it will kill him. It will have to wait until another car comes. Then it will take that to follow us. It will kill the people . . . It has to catch us. We have its weapon!"

"But how—" chattered Norma, "h-how did it know—?"

Burt said bitterly: "It knows all my memories. It can work out how I'll think. It can figure out the choices I'll make. What I'll do—where I'll go—whether I stay on this road or dodge aside . . ."

The car went roaring onward through the night. Trees, hillsides, open fields, appeared for an instant and were gone.

A long time later, winking headlights appeared behind. They were not often visible. They blinked into view and vanished again. Sometimes they were not seen for minutes on end.

When they reappeared, though, they were always a little nearer.

They turned their car again, and again, and yet again. Norma finally grasped the necessity of introducing randomness into their choice of possible paths. She said, "Right" or "left" or "straight ahead" when time for a new choice turned up.

A long time later they drove beside a rushing, foaming mountain stream, under trees which arched completely over the narrow highway. Now and again the headlights glared out over the speeding water. Now and again they could look up and see vast mountain-flanks silhouetted against the star-filled sky overhead.

The road curved and climbed steeply, and they were riding into a very small town indeed, and there was a barrier with a red lantern on it, and half a dozen cars bunched beyond it, and people standing about. A state trooper flagged them to a stop. His hand was grimly at his pistol-holster until he had peered into the car and had seen both Burt's and Norma's faces.

"All traffic's stopped," he said curtly. "There's a maniac running loose in a car. Roads aren't safe. You'll be all right here. Stick around."

Burt nodded, and steered the car to a place among the others. He stopped it. Norma said in a whisper:

"Should we say anything?"

"No," Burt told her. "What we have to say wouldn't be believed here. But it might reach the newspapers. We'd be suspected of mania—especially with that bank loot in the back! We talk to the FBI and nobody else."

He looked keenly out at the people from the other stopped cars. There were a dozen or more, talking uneasily in groups. Now and again a voice came abruptly from the short-wave set in the trooper's car. That would be state police headquarters.

It was two-thirty in the morning, and very cool. The town was a very small one indeed—no more than twenty or thirty houses and two stores. But two highways crossed in it, and the state trooper was halting all traffic on both. Burt considered. He got out to learn the news. Norma came with him.

They listened. The waiting motorists talked in hushed tones. They told each other, over and over, the grisly tale of murder. The maniac had started his career when he killed a filling-station attendant in a small town. Somebody'd just learned that the bank had been robbed there! The dead motorist's wife had described the maniac as pale as death, with glittering eyes and possessed of incredible strength. Thirty miles east the maniac had gone into a service area, killed a diner-cook and a gas attendant, and then waited for another car to turn in. Four men were in the car. The maniac killed two, crippled a third, and the fourth fled into the darkness. The survivors' description of the maniac—who had gone away eastward in their car—confirmed the first account. One of them used a telephone in the diner to report the atrocity. Four dead there, one injured. There was further alerting of all state police-cars.

A trooper found a car abandoned. It was the one taken from the four men of whom two had been killed. It had run out of gas. The bodies of a man and woman were found nearby. Apparently they had stopped to offer help, the maniac had killed them, and then it had gone on in their car.

When they heard where this last event had happened, Burt and Norma tensed. They'd turned off the main highway. The alien had followed, infallibly. Burt had made the decision to turn. The alien had made the same decision.

It had crashed into a police-car set to block a highway. The trooper died, there. The creature had evidently secured another car, because a dead man was found with no car to account for his presence. And a car had gone around the wreckage, out again on the soft shoulder of the road.

That had taken place along the exact line of Burt's and Norma's flight. Cold prickles went down Burt's spine when he heard where that happened! The alien had unerringly followed four successive choices of right-or-left turns, made by Burt. It could anticipate what choices Burt would make, from its analysis of his past experiences. But the last few decisions had been Norma's. And the alien could not tell what she would choose. Whether to take a right or a left-hand branching of a highway. Whether to take the shortest route to a destination or a longer one. These decisions did not follow the pattern Burt's mind would have made. The creature from space could not tell what they would be.

Which, of course, was unquestionably why they had not been overtaken.

The short-wave speaker in the trooper's car spoke in staccato fashion:

"All cars . . . All cars . . . Ten minutes ago a car traveling eighty miles an hour ran into a traffic barricade at Coytesville. It smashed the barrier, the driver lost control, and the car swerved into an empty-store-building and caught fire. It is now burning with the building. This may be the maniac. Caution will be continued, but this may be the man . . ."

Buzzing talk all around the barricade. It sounded right. Only a maniac would drive a car eighty miles an hour at night, so he couldn't stop at a red-lighted barricade. If the maniac had been killed in the crash and his body burned in the building, it served him right. People talked more loudly, while Burt and Norma listened. They were relieved. How many had he killed? Two at the first filling station, four at the second, a man and a woman, a state trooper and another man. Ten people killed by one maniac in a night's orgy of madness. But it must have been the maniac who'd been killed, because only a maniac would drive eighty miles an hour and through a red-lighted barricade.

Which was true, but there are maniacs and maniacs.

Time passed, and they waited, and there were no further reports of atrocities. It seemed more and more likely that the murderous creature had been killed and his body burned in a car and an empty store-building. Some of the motorists grew impatient. Burt did not. He moved about at the edge of the grouping of waiting people. There was a wire-strand fence at the side of the road. One strand was broken. The loose end trailed. An idea came to Burt.

82

He broke off th snapped wire, by bending it repeatedly at one place. It was stout, stiff fence-wire. He trailed seven or eight feet of it back to the car. He took out a pair of pliers. He snipped off a short length of wire and wrapped it once around the alien's weapon—and twisted the end. He repeated the process. He began to enclose the cryptic device in a series of tightly-drawn, tightly-twisted lengths of wire, any one of which would prevent pressure on any operating-stud underneath it, and all of which would prevent the device from being used at all until the wire covering had been removed, strand by strand.

The tiny hamlet about them slept soundly. There were seven cars waiting for assurance of safety. But the short-wave report did sound as if all danger was over. It seemed extremely plausible that the maniac—or the alien from space— had been killed and his body destroyed in a burned-down empty store-building.

But Burt had had a shock. The alien had followed his choices of ways to go. It was possible, at least, that it had been able to anticipate that Burt would ultimately make Norma choose the way he drove. If that were true—at the moment when knowing Burt's mind would do no good—the alien would abandon the direct chase. It would go on to something else. It would not abandon its emergency weapon. It could not.

But it could know exactly how Burt would react.

He thought very grimly as he finished encasing the weapon. The alien could not anticipate that. It couldn't reason that Burt would find a loose fence-wire and have time to make use of it to make the weapon useless—for a time, at least. But there had to be a decision the alien could anticipate, which it would do it no good to know in advance. It would be completely implacable. It had to have its weapon back. It couldn't be allowed to have it. So it had to be trapped and killed, once and for all.

There was one decision it would do the alien no good to be able to foresee. Burt lifted his head from where he worked on the weapon.

"Norma," he said quietly, "You've got to make a plan. Good or bad, it doesn't matter. But it has to be yours. Now listen . . ."

He talked quietly. Presently there was a staccato noise from the trooper's car—the short-wave set. When it ended, there were stirrings. Burt got out as one of the waiting cars droned into low and started off along the highway. Others were whirring their starters. Burt asked questions. The fire had been put out and the body of the man in the eighty-mile car had been examined. He was a big man, six feet and over in height. He should have been a powerful man. He could have been capable of the maniac's atrocities. Traffic was permitted to move, again.

Burt went back and took the wheel.

"It wasn't the creature, but a human being," he told Norma. "The creature's bound to be hiding now. It'll be waiting for us. Where?"

Gray dawn began, and it was a matter of only ten or fifteen miles to the town where both Burt and Norma lived. Before them, on a narrow highway, there was a long procession of clumsy, make-shift, slatted farm-trucks. Burt came up to the last of them and glanced at Norma. She shook her head slightly. He fell in behind the line, not trying to pass. She said:

"I feel foolish, telling you what to do."

Burt said carefully: "The creature can figure out every decision I'll make, including the decision that it can figure out what I'll decide. But it doesn't know what you'll decide. So you know what we want to do, and you're deciding the moves toward it. That is the one way to outguess the creature."

Norma protested: "But we're betting our lives on acting illogically."

They were. In order to have any real hope of living on, Burt and Norma had to convince somebody—the FBI preferably—that the alien was real and what he was, and that he simply must be captured. Obviously, they must produce that belief without giving the thing from space a chance to kill them first. Since he knew their purpose and had—to put it mildly—no scruples at all, the last item was difficult. Their danger was not one particle less than it had been. The alien was infernally intelligent, and its desperation was complete. It would even risk detection to get its weapon back, because its enemies might not ever learn of its landing, but it could not survive on earth unarmed. Because it was not human!

The car trailed the odorous line of farm-trucks toward the city. The dawnlight strengthened. Presently Burt said somberly:

"The thing'll have changed its appearance by now. It knows it can't go on when everybody screams as soon as they see it."

"But it's color-blind! What can it do?"

"It's got my memories," said Burt bitterly. "It'll think of sun-glasses to hide its eyes—and there's at least one pair in nearly every car's glove-compartment. It'll think of a false beard to hide its face and mouth. I'd be willing to bet that somewhere there's been a beauty-salon window smashed so somebody could snatch a wig off a mannikin. It could make a beard. I wore a false one, once, in amateur theatricals! I'll bet I could describe it by now. Soft hat pulled down low. Long coat and beard. Dark glasses. Probably a cane or a crutch to walk with. It'll figure out that it can't just melt into the human race and have nobody look at it. You notice unusual things about a commonplace man—pallor, or anything else. But in an unusual figure, the odd is commonplace!"

He glowered. Norma said hopefully:

"Do you realize that though it can know what you do because it knows all your experiences, you can know what it'll do because you know every bit of information it has about Earth?"

Burt blinked. He thought it over. Then he brightened.

"I hadn't thought of it that way! But it's so! And it puts a new light on things! Hmm."

Daylight was here, now, and very far away they could just see the tall buildings of the city which was their home, rising from the smoky mist that seems to cover most cities at dawning. A little way ahead a neat secondary road led off to the right, away from where it was Burt's instinct and purpose to go, and where the alien should expect to meet him. The market-trucks rumbled ahead a little more swiftly now. But when Burt reached that minor highway, he turned aside with a new decisiveness. He drove not toward the city, but toward a suburban town some twenty miles away which he chose because he had never been there in his life before, and the creature from emptiness could not possibly find it in his memories.

As he stepped cheerfully on the gas, the sun lifted from the horizon and all the world and wide green fields looked beautifully alive and sparkling.

His activities, he explained gravely to Norma, were deliberate folly, because the alien couldn't imagine such a thing. They had breakfast at an inn, whose earliest customers they were. They lingered over the meal—though as a matter of pure precaution Burt sat where he could watch the doorway and out the windows. Here he secured writing materials and wrote a moderately lengthy note, with much careful choice of phrasing. When the first stores opened, Burt bought a good-sized suitcase, a flat metal box, an assortment of fishermen's sinkers, and a hunting-knife. Then he drove to a newly opened garage and packed the sinkers in the metal box and had the box brazed shut, all around, so it couldn't be opened again without metal-cutting tools. While the brazing-torch flamed, he went in the back part of the car—his nostrils wrinkled momentarily—and packed the suitcase. He packed it with the bag the alien had brought from the robbed bank. With money. He included the note he'd written with the bag.

Then he found a messenger service and dispatched the carefully locked suitcase by special messenger on an interurban bus. Norma followed him unquestioningly about while he did these cryptic errands.

"Now," he told her when the messenger had started off, "there's just one thing more, besides the phone-calls I'm going to make presently."

"I don't understand in the least," said Norma uneasily. "I know what you've done, but not why."

"The natural thing for me to do," explained Burt, "would be sensible. Go straight to the FBI at daybreak. Spout my stuff. Show my proofs. I'd go direct to their headquarters, because I wouldn't expect them to believe my yarn and come to me. The creature knows that I am highly intelligent—" he grinned—"so it expects me to be sensible. But I know what it knows, so I'm doing foolish things to confuse it. There's one more thing to do."

He told her. She gasped.

"But it's ridiculous!" she protested. "I never heard of such a thing!"

"You just have," Burt corrected her gently. "Come along."

They had to stand in line. She still protested that it was foolish. But not very energetically.

They drove into their home town at late dusk. Burt had had several conferences with the FBI by telephone. His messenger had delivered the brand-new suitcase to the FBI during the early morning. Opened, the suitcase contained eighteen thousand dollars, robbed from a bank the night before, nearly two hundred miles away. With it there was a note. By the time Burt telephoned, the FBI was intensely curious and almost inclined to believe a wild tale—but his story was much wilder than they'd expected. But it linked up with the activities of a maniac during the previous night. It coincided with three items in the local police news of early morning. A beauty-shop window had been smashed and a mannikin's wig stolen. A second-hand clothing shop had been robbed. A store for orthopedic appliances broken into. But it was Burt's story that made the orthopedic store discover that one crutch had been stolen with the contents of its cash register.

When a chemist reported on a scrap of brown plastic Burt had enclosed, the FBI was staggered. It began to hunt for somebody—some human—who should have answered Burt's description. They found nobody. They began to be dubious. But half an hour before Burt's return they suddenly became convinced. There was an hotel just opposite the building in which the FBI offices were. In late afternoon one of the housekeepers entered a guest's room and happened to open a closet. She found there the body of a chambermaid. The maid's neck was broken. The occupant—checked in only that morning—had been a bent and whiskered cripple of convincingly feeble appearance.

It could be guessed that the maid had noticed that his appearance was not wholly human, and had stared at him.

So, as Burt entered the edge of town, a car pulled up alongside his and a man in the car made a recognition signal. Burt felt a little better, but not much. The alien hadn't been caught. It had to be. It looked like it wouldn't be until Burt caught it, and he was grim about that necessity.

So he drove through the dusk and the city traffic to the building where Norma lived. There were shadows in the air and the street lights winked on as he drove. The smell of dust and hot asphalt and gasoline fumes, and a whiff of green stuff, and the sound of people in motion with all their contrivances.

He drove sedately to Norma's address. Night had fallen swiftly, and it was dark when he parked. He saw a movement in the shadows nearby. Distinct cold shadows ran up and down his spine. But then a figure made an agreed-on recognition signal. He felt better. At least one FBI man. He hoped more.

There were. He and Norma went inside. She was pale. She started a little when she saw a strange elevator-operator. But Burt felt a warm gratitude. It would be his inevitable instinct to take Norma to her home first of all. Before he went to his own apartment. Before he went to the FBI.

In the elevator, the man nodded when Burt looked questioningly at him. The elevator stopped at Norma's floor. They got out and Burt automatically followed her lead down the hall. But suddenly he got ahead of her, and sniffed, and then he said very quietly:

"This is your door?"

She nodded, deathly white. He turned her away from it and gave her a little shove—so she'd go away and let him enter by himself. She'd already given him her key. He put it in the lock and turned it and opened the door—unobtrusively turning the catch so the door could be opened from outside, behind him—and reached in to where Norma had said the light-switch was.

The room leaped into light. Empty. Burt went in. The door closed decisively behind him, and Norma was there with him. She wouldn't be left behind. The faint, faint, inhuman smell was stronger.

As if the closing of the door had been a signal, the alien came from an inner room. It had a revolver in its hand. It wore a shapeless soft black hat, and a long coat. It had a long and silky beard But it took off its dark glasses and threw them away. It said tonelessly—in Burt's own voice:

"Give me my weapon."

Burt did not have to feign surprise. The emotional impact of facing the creature was enough. But he slowly reached into his pocket and brought out the brazed-shut metal box. He tossed it on a table near the creature. He said grimly:

"I didn't want it to go off by accident."

The alien picked up the box. Its plastic fingers tore at it. The box did not yield. It pocketed the box and moved—

Burt presented the hunting-knife, drawn and ready. He was completely savage and completely the match of the alien in ferocity, because Norma was here. The alien stopped short and said without expression:

"I would have killed you silently."

Its revolver came up. Burt snapped off the light and flung Norma aside as two shots crashed in the darkness and the gun clicked empty. Then there was a raging humming noise, wholly unlike any sound that could have been made by a human throat—and the door burst in and flashlight beams darted inward. Burt said sharply:

"That's it!"

The thing stared at the FBI men. It hummed horribly. Then it flung its useless pistol at them with superhuman force and scrambled with incredible agility for the window. It crashed through to the fire-escape. It vanished as the FBI men plunged after it. A hand thrust a flashlight out. There were shoutings. A shot outside. The three men climbed out. One of them started up. There was another shot outside, and whistlings, and there were flickerings of light, and a loud humming noise that had somehow the effect of a scream of fury, only infinitely more terrible to hear.

A man shrieked. There were shots overhead. A fusillade . . .

The man who came back to the apartment looked acutely ill. He held the metal box gingerly in his hands. It was twisted and bent. A monstrous strength had been exerted upon it, and a brazed seam had begun to give.

"We got it up on the roof," said the FBI man, in the tone of a man talking about something he will have bad dreams about for a long time to come. "It broke one man's arm, but it kept trying to open this box even while we were pumping bullets into it. It came out of that human skin like it was a cocoon, worrying at this box and making that humming noise. What was it?"

Burt was very busy, but he said politely:

"I haven't the least idea what it would be called."

"Listen!" said the FBI man, sweating. "We didn't really believe you, but that money, and then the maid being killed and all—" Burt looked politely annoyed. The FBI man said, "This is—the bomb, isn't it? It almost got at it."

Burt removed one arm from where it was and produced the creature's weapon, elaborately sheathed with twisted wire.

"No. This is the weapon. I didn't want to take a chance of anybody fiddling with it. It goes to Washington. Atomic Energy Commission. Tell them about the creature."

The FBI man took the weapon in a trembling hand.

"We'll tell them about the—thing, whatever it was," he said sickishly. "We'll tell them! My God, did you ever see anything like that in your life?"

"No," said Burt. "I didn't. I'd rather not, anyhow. Look! I don't know what your name is, but could we talk this over in the morning? We just got married today and my wife's rather overwrought. Could you excuse us?"

The FBI man said, "Yeah. Oh, sure!" He went to the door and said: "Until we get orders from Washington, we won't let any news get out. You understand? For the moment, no talking?"

"No talking," agreed Burt. "Goodnight."

"Goodnight," said the FBI man. He went out the door. He couldn't remember which of the two objects was the one to be careful of, and he had no clear idea what the thing could do anyhow—except that the creature on the roof had been trying to get at it while it hummed and died. So the FBI man walked very gingerly down the hall carrying both objects very carefully. He walked like a man carrying an atomic bomb.

He was.

Anthropological Note

THE MEETING of Miss Cummings and Ray Hale in a Krug village on Venus is one of those events for which there is no real explanation. Unless one believes that there was or is a Th'Tark, who arranged the matter, it simply doesn't make sense. But it did happen. Miss Cummings met Hale under quite preposterous circumstances in a female-Krug village. She had known him before, a good many years since and forty million miles away. Then she had passionately wished for sudden death to strike him. When, after years, she saw him again she knew the same wish and what followed very probably prevented the extermination of the Krug in the name of the prosperity of interplanetary commerce. This would amount to a proof of Th'Tark's interest—if there ever was a Th'Tark. But it's all very complicated.

Th'Tark is or was the possibly mythical Law-giver of the Krug, who are the quasi-semi-humanoid inhabitants of the Krug Archipelago in the Summer Sea on Venus. They look more human than most earthly primates, probably because they aren't furry, and Th'Tark is said to have set up their laws and customs and very dubious moral code some tens of thousands of Venusian years ago. It was Th'Tark who decreed that male Krug should live dispirited, gloomy lives in the jungles by the seashore while female Krug built villages, practiced agriculture and other useful arts, and raised children. Miss Cummings was the lady anthropologist who examined their culture and kept them from extermination.

She landed in their midst from a survey-ship offshore from an island which on the map is called Tanit. The morning of her arrival was quite ordinary. There was no sunrise, of course. There never is. There was blackness everywhere at first, and then the sky became ever-so-faintly gray, and the cloudbank overhead lightened by imperceptible degrees, and presently it was morning with leaping waves all about the ship and foaming surf on the beaches and at the foot of the cliffs of the island a mile away. She prepared to land alone, as a field expedition in anthropology with qualified assistants in the base, which was the ship. Her purpose was pure science, but the reason was interplanetary trade.

Venus wasn't well-settled then, and the cost of transportation to Earth was so high that only very precious things indeed could stand the cost and show a profit. But in the Krug Archipelago such a product had been found. It was *crythli* pearls and pearl-shell. They were utterly beautiful and utterly past imitation. They were the most desirable gems that men had ever seen, and their value was fabulous. But the few—still extremely rare—specimens which had been found had been discovered in the possession of male Krug in the jungles. The Krug were not anxious to part with them. They mentioned Th' Tark and females—the latter very reluctantly—and shut up. Moreover, when a Krug began to gather *crythli* shell and pearls, it was a sign that shortly he would disappear. Permanently. So trade in *crythli* pearls and pearl-shell languished, and the economic status of the Venusian colony needed interplanetary exchange. Hence Miss Cummings.

On this particular morning a helicopter lifted heavily from the ship and droned toward the island. Miss Cummings was in a landing-basket slung below. At four thousand feet altitude she could see the whole island, ringed by foam, with high mountains and broad valleys in its interior. The copter skimmed sharp-edged mountain-peaks and then settled down and down into the valley where a chosen village lay. The village had been studied by telephotography from the air, and Miss Cummings already had a fascinating list of questions to be answered. Why, for example, were there only females and Krug-children in the village? No picture had showed any male older than what would be earliest teen-age in a human. Was it true that the larger, kraal-like thatched dwellings belonged to multiparous lady Krug, while the curiously incomplete circle of quite small houses belonged to hopeful maidens? And those small, rounded, flower-beds before the kraal-houses. Filter-photography insisted that they were tastefully bordered with *crythli* shell, used by the Krug as clam-shells are sometimes used by the owners of beach-cottages on Earth. If this were true, they were fabulously valuable and the prosperity of the human colony on Venus required that they be acquired—by peaceful means if possible, but acquired—for shipment back to Earth.

Miss Cummings knew the blissful anticipation of a lady anthropologist with a new culture to study and assurance of credit for the job. She was utterly happy as the copter droned on down to land her for the beginning of her research. Of all things and persons in the solar system, she thought least of Ray Hale. But he was of paramount importance to her job, actually. As she watched the sprawling, thatched-roof village enlarge at her approach, Hale was doing some research, too. That very same morning, in fact. But his methods were his own.

He had quite a reputation, had Hale. The colonial government had learned of his arrival on Venus just too late to grab him before he vanished into unexplored territory. He wasn't welcome on a newly colonized planet. He'd caused the First Native War on Mars, by taking advantage of the fact that at that time human law had not defined the killing of Martians as murder. He was responsible for the B'setse Massacre on Titan, when a hundred and fifty human colonists died as the result of his treatment of the most ancient and therefore richest of the Titanian natives nearby. He got away with rich loot from Titan, as he had on Mars, but colonial government officials didn't want him around.

On this particular morning, not three hundred miles from where Miss Cummings landed, he was doing research in his own fashion. He'd caught a male Krug and was extracting information from him. Traders after *crythli* shell had developed a sort of pidgin-Krug with which limited communication was possible, and Hale used that as part of his process. The rest of it would not be nice to describe. But he was forcing his captive to try to tell him, by an inadequate means of communication, facts he probably didn't know about mysteries he almost certainly didn't understand and positively didn't like to think about.

It was an extremely revolting performance, and it lasted a long time, but Hale probably enjoyed it. He was still a fairly handsome man—his good looks had been important in the affair causing Miss Cummings' passionate desire for lightning to strike him—but he wasn't at all attractive as he worked on the Krug. The whole business was ghastly, but Th'Tark probably allowed it. After all, it bore upon the preservation of the Krug race and culture from extermination.

In any case, when Hale finally killed the Krug and washed the debris overboard from the deck of his stolen boat, he knew where *crythli* shells were found. But he didn't think of looking for them himself. Instead, he took other information the Krug had yielded, and rather zestfully worked out a pattern for action which should yield him all the *crythli* pearls a man could want. The shell itself was precious, as mother-of-pearl had been, but the pearls themselves were more precious a thousand times over.

Three hundred miles away, Miss Cummings arrived at the chosen village. The helicopter circled that straggling settlement and a small horde of Krug swarmed out to stare up at it. Maybe they thought Th'Tark had something to do with it. (Maybe Th'Tark had.) They stared up—almost exclusively female. The exceptions were children—boy-Krug. The copter settled gently until the landing-basket touched ground. Miss Cummings cast off. The copter rose to the cloud-bank overhead where Th'Tark was reputed to dwell, and remained handy to come back within two minutes if Miss Cummings called for it by communicator. She had a small, nearly invisible hand-weapon with which to hold Krug off that long if necessary.

She didn't need to. The villagers approached her warily. But they observed that she was female. She had adopted a costume which emphasized the Krugoid features of a human woman. She held up gifts. Beaming, she offered them.

In five minutes she informed the copter crew that she wouldn't need them, but they stayed overhead anyhow just in case.

The business of making friends went on swimmingly. Miss Cummings was beautifully equipped for field investigation of a female social system. Before coming to Venus she'd taught denatured anthropology to classes of human college girls. She knew her females. For example, the older matrons of the Krug village had exactly the authoritative and self-satisfied air of a committee of college alumnae. They were middle-aged or older and accustomed to having their own way under all circumstances. To them Miss Cummings was charmingly deferential. There was one awkward moment, but it soon passed over. Miss Cummings, trying to begin speech, pointed to some object and used the trade-Krug male language word for it. Her audience tittered. Miss Cummings knew instantly that male and female Krug spoke different languages—as in some primitive cultures on Earth—and it was indecorous for one sex to use a noun or verb appropriate to the other. But Miss Cummings made no other break. The younger females, she observed, wore the impatient expression of human college girls. She addressed them cheerfully. To the older matrons she distributed necklaces of fluorescent beads and to the younger she passed out bracelets and small mirrors. The young females thereupon treated her with the tolerant condescension the young give to the older in all races without exception.

She even dealt adequately with the children. Mature Krug wore crudely woven garments, but the Krug-children were as innocent of clothing as of guile. To them she distributed sweetmeats. Not candy, of course. Krug taste-buds are not like human ones. She passed out bonbons of almost pure quinine and the Krug-children went into ecstasies over the luxury. But Miss Cummings discovered that the community did not approve the wasting of such things upon boys. Only future Krug matrons were worthy of largesse.

By nightfall Miss Cummings had been accepted as a welcome visitor and assigned one of the smaller houses in the incomplete circle which from air-photos had been considered the maïdens' houses. Next day she set to work to acquire a vocabulary.

Hale—a shade under three hundred miles away, now—caught a second Krug male. This time he chose one of the youngest of those dispirited creatures who loaf and lurk in the jungles of the Krug islands. This creature he treated gently, at intervals, plying him with quinine and alternate beatings and cajolings. He got from him—and recorded for study—the female-language words which the younger Krug remembered more fully than an older one would have done. It was a racking experience for the adolescent Krug. He'd been kicked out of his village and stridently told to go and associate with the other worthless males in the jungle. He was embittered. But Hale made him recall and repeat all his childhood experiences. In the end he kicked his second captive ashore and prepared to make use of the data he'd acquired. He had no faintest desire to perform any action for the preservation of the Krug race. It just happened that way —though only Th'Tark could possibly have thought of it in advance. *If* there is a Th'Tark.

At the end of a week in the village, Miss Cummings was in an anthropologist's idea of heaven. She was doing the first known research on an extensive race-culture, and she had skilled help on the steamer, and she would get all the credit. But the help was important. For example, the Krug language required careful analysis. Not only were there male and female versions which were wholly unlike, but there were honorific terms as in Japanese, which could have been pitfalls. Different forms of address were used to different Krug matrons according to whether they had one or two or more children up to a dozen, after which a super-honorific applied. This could have caused trouble.

With the research staff on the ship, however, she learned to speak with remarkable speed. Up to a certain point. At a definite place she ran into frustration. As a human being, Miss Cummings could never fully believe that the Krug language had no word meaning *why?* The lack of it was like a blank stone wall preventing progress. Her communicator sent all her gathered information to the ship, with her comments.

The phiologists labored over it. In long discussions between ship and village, Miss Cummings led in the discovery that the language had only one gender (female) but all personal pronouns had thirty-two forms, honorific or self-deprecatory. There was an incredibly complex system of verb-conjugations, and a fine and adequate vocabulary of nouns. But all the nouns were proper ones! The word which meant *tree* meant *this tree*. There was no word for the abstract notion of tree-ness which was common to all arborescent plants. Therefore there was no verbal machinery for the operations of logic.

On the face of it, the fact was impossible. The Krug were civilized in their fashion, and they definitely used speech to convey objective information. But they did not discuss. They did not argue. They were invincibly literal-minded, and therefore they were probably quite happy. But Miss Cummings was not pleased when she asked about this custom and that—and the framing of a question was a tortuous process —and received the bland and irrelevant reply that she was this-unmarried-female. She couldn't ask why her status prevented her being told. There was no *why*. It was definitely a female culture.

She seethed. She almost resented her unmarried state, since it prevented the pursuance of anthropological research. With the peculiar jealousy of a woman scientific worker, she began to envision a married woman being hastily supplied with the data she'd compiled and then sent in to replace her. It could be said that she burned.

Th'Tark could have told her to be at ease, of course, if anybody could. If the Krug were to escape extermination by the march of progress, Miss Cummings had to be responsible. Because she knew Ray Hale.

He'd gathered quite a lot of information she didn't have, by the time the language difficulty had reached its most frustrating form for her. Before she'd been in the village more than two weeks, Hale had acquired close to a quart of *crythli* pearls—and no trader had ever before been able to gather as many as half a dozen in one trading-season from the Krug. Some of those that Hale acquired were rather crude-ly pierced for stringing, but he was well over a millionaire in *crythli* pearls, already, and they'd only cost him a couple of weeks of research and a few hair-raising moments and a crime most men would queasily prefer not to commit. But it wasn't murder, because Krug hadn't yet been ruled human— under the laws forbidding homicide.

In her third week in the village, Miss Cummings witnessed a partial parallel to Hale's enterprise, though she didn't know it.

It began at daybreak, when she was wakened by the morning-noises. There were snickering, giggling noises from the jungle, which was only a hundred yards from the incomplete circle of maidens'-huts. There were boomings deeper in among the trees, and something honked discordantly, and something else made sounds as if of hysterical laughter. But Miss Cummings was used to such sounds now. They were commonplace. The noises that disturbed her were speech-sounds.

There were chitterings which were children—boys and females together. There were deeper, authoritative, firm notes which were those of matrons. There was a great congregation of the village near Miss Cummings' house.

She dressed herself and went out-of-doors. All the village was assembled in the center of the maidens'-huts ring. The unmarried-females were gathered together, and they fairly jittered with hopeful agitation. The Krug-children raced and scampered about a solemn group of the older females. Miss Cummings approached, with her communicator turned on and relaying everything to the tape-recorders on the ship. As she drew near, she saw that a *crythli* shell was being passed from hand to hand among the older matrons. They examined it with great care and extreme minuteness. They acted, indeed, like short-sighted alumnae caught without their eye-glasses and seeming rather to smell than to look at some interesting object.

The oldest, stoutest female—possessed of a preposterous number of offspring—seemed to debate a very long time. The maidens jittered more visibly than before. Then the oldest female solemnly handed the *crythli*-shell to one of them. The maiden clasped it to her breast with dramatic satisfaction. This particular young female stood out in Miss Cummings' mind because in a Kruggish way she resembled a frog-like undergraduate who'd infested one of Miss Cummings' classes at her woman's college on Earth. That undergraduate, with thick spectacles and buck teeth and an irritating personality, had been married the day after graduation to a millionaire. It had seemed injustice at the time. Now her Krug opposite number was plainly chosen for some splendid prize. The *crythli* shell, incidentally, would have fetched a good fifteen thousand credits in Venus City, and several times that on Earth.

A gabbling uproar rose, and the other maidens looked bitter over their contemporary's triumph. The matrons gathered about the chosen one, beaming at her. The Krug children burst into a run for the jungle. They vanished in its depths.

Miss Cummings fumed because all this was inexplicable and she couldn't ask the question, "Why?"

The morning passed. Miss Cummings, in her hut, conferred with her aides and superiors on the ship offshore. Whatever was coming, it was without precedent in this research. Therefore it must be important. She was urged not to miss any developments.

She went out as the village children returned from the jungle. They carried burdens. There were logs of the hollow, cane-like jungle-trees which broke off cleanly at their joints, They were of diverse lengths and thicknesses. Other children staggered under loads of jungle-leaves and vines and creepers. They marched to that part of the village where the kraal-like dwelling stood. They began to construct a new house.

This was as remarkable as anything else about the whole Krug culture. No adult supervised. No instructions were issued. The children swarmed about the enterprise like so many bees, and if Miss Cummings had not been engaged in getting barred from all the matrons and the frog-faced Krug girl, she would have gaped as the house went up. Because it was done perfectly. With a precision they could not possibly have learned, the Krug children heaved the feather-light logs into upright position without even a floor-plan scratched on the gound. They deftly flipped crosspieces into place and tied them with vines. They established a roofing framework in the same fashion and thatched it with absolute competence. Then they stuck limber saplings here and there and began matter-of-factly to thatch down the walls. In a matter of some four hours they had built a house indistinguishable from the kraal-like dwellings of the matrons, only with fewer rooms. But extra rooms could be added.

Having performed the work without instructions, they ceased it without being dismissed. 'Five minutes after it was done they were busy again with the normal and zestful and quite useless occupations of Krug childhood. And perhaps the most astonishing thing about the whole job was that there was neither anything lacking in the house nor any material left over. They'd brought back exactly enough.

It was too much for Miss Cummings to grasp. She was striving to gather information on what she considered more important matters. Barred from the society of the matrons, for today, she visited the other maidens in their huts. She found them occupied as usual. Some of them wove. Miss

Cummings had shown them minor improvements in the process which improved their product, but they ignored her instructions. They used the cloth she'd partly woven, but they did not adopt her changes.

Miss Cummings chatted with them, subject to the limitations of the language. She could say "this-cloth-is-good" or "I-come-to-visit-you." And they could agree. She could observe "the-house-is-becoming," meaning that it was being built. Which was similarly true. She could even say, and did say, "the-maiden-with-the-*crythli*-shell-is-not-where-we-are." They agreed to that, also. But Miss Cummings, bursting with scientific curiosity, could not ask why a new house had been built or where the *crythli* shell had come from or why it was presented to the frog-like maiden and what it signified. The language blocked all efforts.

Roy Hale could have told her, though. He was only two hundred miles away, then, and he now had three quarts of *crythli* pearls and did not even bother to own more than a few shells—though practically any shell was worth ten thousand credits in Venus City. He was a multi-multi-millionaire in *crythli* pearls, and still he planned to grow richer. He considered it humorous that there was no law forbidding his enterprise. It had not been defined that Krug were human, and therefore there was no penalty for killing them.

But to Miss Cummings the matter was still mystery. A *crythli* shell in the center of the maidens'-hut ring. The gift of the shell to the especially repulsive Krug girl. The building of a house. The complete withdrawal into privacy of the Krug maiden and all the matrons. Miss Cummings made wild guesses and waited for something to happen to solve the mystery.

She had to wait until evening—until the cloudbank overhead began faintly to dim, since there were no sunsets on Venus. The light was no more than halfway faded when the Krug girl came out of the newly built kraal-house. Miss Cummings saw her and fairly sputtered her excitement into the communicator.

The Krug girl sat down before the new house with an air of elaborate unconcern. Always, previously, she had worn the single crude cloth garment of her sister-maidens. Now she wore a quite special outfit of which Miss Cummings had had no inkling before. But being a woman she grasped its marvelousness and its meaning instantly. The Krug girl was dressed as a bride. But no human bride was ever arrayed in a headdress of *crythli* pearls which would have sold for millions on the Earth-market, nor wore necklaces of *crythli* pearls no mere millionaire could have hoped to buy, nor did any human bride ever wear armlets and belts and breast-plates of *crythli* shell, when a reasonably rich man's wife only hoped wistfully to own a single small shell disk.

Miss Cummings gasped the news into the communicator. She was about to witness, she said agitatedly, the marriage ceremony of the Krug. It must be! It was the more certain because there was no visible bridegroom!

The village gathered. Behind the gaudily decorated Krug girl the matrons of the village took their places. They were stout and bland and infinitely satisfied with themselves and all the world. They looked rather like an alumnae group posing for a photograph on their twentieth class reunion. As the cloudbank overhead became darker and darker and more nearly black, there was a hushed waiting atmosphere everywhere. The children appeared. They came filing out in a long line. The foremost—a Krug child barely toddling—carried a lighted torch with tremendous solicitude. The others carried things which might also be torches, but were unlighted. There was silence save for the noises of the nearby jungle. The cloudbank darkened and darkened, and presently it was truly night. There was no light anywhere in the village except the one small torch in the hands of a toddling Krug child. And nothing happened for a very long time.

Then came crisp, grunting commands from the oldest of the matrons. The small child reached its light to the next. A second torch flamed. That torch swung to a third, and that to a fourth, and so on until fifty flaring, sparkling flames furnished a brighter light than Miss Cummings had ever seen in the village after nightfall.

Then, and only then, she saw the bridegroom. In the darkness, guided by the first and only burning torch, the male Krug had crept into the village and to the new house. He had doubtless been perceived, but Th'Tark had undoubtedly ordained that a pretense of invisibility should rule until he stood before his bride.

Now he seemed to shrivel in the torchlight. He appeared at once desperately to wish to be anywhere else on the planet—in which he was like many human bridegrooms—and despairingly to be resigned to his fate. In the torchlight, seeming numbed in some fashion, he unburdened himself of *crythli* shells. He laid them down, one by one, before the adorned but stonily unresponsive maiden. Shell after shell to a fabulous value was piled before her. He actually laid down a full two dozen of the gleaming things. Most human

99

girls would have grown starry-eyed if presented with a single one.

He straightened up. The torchlight glistened on his body. Miss Cummings had an impression that he sweated like a man in absolute terror and despair.

The most ancient of the matrons grunted.

The seated, decorated Krug-bride looked scornfully upon the despised male. But, very, very condescendingly, she rose. She faced him. Then she reached out her hand and with a sort of infinite and conscious generosity she touched him. Which act of abandoning aversion appeared to be the official climax of the wedding.

There was a clamor. The children dashed their torches to the ground and stamped on them. The village reverted to darkness. Miss Cummings heard rustlings all about her as if the inhabitants of the village returned to their homes, the ceremony over.

She made her own way to her own maidens'-circle hut and settled down zestfully for a long conference over the communicator. She reported the wedding with the enthusiasm and rapturous sentimentality of a lady society reporter at the wedding of a human heiress to an Earth-Council member. She gloated over the bride's costume. Being a woman she considered the relative insignificance of the bridegroom and his total lack of male attendants a right and proper thing. She was even sentimental about the symbolism of the bride's formally excepting this one male from her abhorrence of masculine creation.

Presently she calmed down enough to talk proper anthropological shop. The absence of other males from the village population remained odd, but there were references to analogous social customs on Earth. There was a Himalayan culture in which after marriage there was a honeymoon lasting only three days, when the bride and bridegroom separated for most of a year before setting up housekeeping together. There was an Indo-Chinese culture in which females affected to ignore the existence of males for an almost indefinite period, remaining in their parental home until the bride's parents insisted that their daughter's husband take over the support of his by-then-numerous offspring. There were many human customs suggested by this Krug wedding. There was enthusiastic anthropological shop-talk on the ether-waves of Venus, that night.

Next morning Miss Cummings happily noted that the bride appeared in her usual costume—with only a little more cloth added to it in token of her matronly status—and joined the matrons in their activities. She was addressed by a new honorific, and all the personal pronouns appropriate to an unmarried girl were now changed in her speech and in speech to her. But her husband did not appear at all. Miss Cummings had almost expected it.

There was one other interesting item. Miss Cummings got up at the break of day, but not in time to see the ornamentation of the mounded, rounded flower-bed now existing before the home of the new matron. It had quite two dozen *crythli* shells disposed about it, but of course the flowers were not yet established. They had been planted, though.

Miss Cummings and her aides on the ship discussed the matter exhaustively. The *crythli*-shell gift of the bridegroom had its parallel in bride-prices paid on Earth. There had possibly been an additional gift of pearls which Miss Cummings had not observed. The use of precious shells to decorate a flower-bed was conspicuous waste like the potlatch festivals of Alaskan Indians. The fact that the bride-gift was without utility-value resembled the old Bornean custom, in which an aspiring lover had to present a new-taken human head to his inamorata, for her to think him a good catch.

The village settled down again. The bride faithfully watered the plants in her shell-bordered flower-garden. She preened herself on her new status. But her husband remained invisible.

Miss Cummings practically forgot about him during the week that followed. A disturbing change in her own status was beginning to appear. She was taking up, now, the distribution of authority in the village, and discovered that the oldest of the matrons had begun to regard her with a disturbing disapproval.

The status of this pompous dowager' was approximately that of headwoman of the village, yet the authority she exercised was not quite that of command. From time to time she gave what could be considered signals for community activity—for cultivating the soil, for repairing the community huts. Everybody worked at whatever she indicated was to be the activity for the day. But she gave no orders. Nobody asked for instructions. Everyone down to the smallest Krug child seemed to know perfectly every duty that might be required. And conversation was strictly confined to observations of objective fact.

When Miss Cummings had been in the village for five weeks, she received a special call from this strutting and authoritative female. The matron-Krug came to Miss Cummings' maiden-hut and regarded her with disapproval. Her

101

air was something like the aloof scorn with which an elderly married alumna, revisiting the college of her youth, looks upon a middle-aged and unmarried professor who seems unlikely to emulate the alumna's career. The stout lady Krug made two statements to Miss Cummings. The first one, the philologists on the ship decided, could be translated as meaning, "you-are-venerable-and-have-no-children." The second would be translated variously as *finish, end, termination,* or practically any word meaning finality. The Krug matron then formally handed Miss Cummings an odd pointed instrument made out of the only really hard wood to grow in the Krug Archipelago. And she waddled out of Miss Cummings' hut.

Miss Cummings, disturbed, transmitted a picture of the instrument to the survey-ship. The anthropological staff was able to determine that it was old, that it was sharp, and that it was enigmatic. Miss Cummings, however, had an intuition. She did not like it.

Here, Miss Cummings' instincts served her better than Ray Hale's methods of research. She could guess what it was for, and he could not. At this time he was less than seventy miles from Miss Cummings' island. He knew more about *crythli* pearls and shell than any other human being. But he didn't know about that instrument.

Miss Cummings guessed indignantly. The Krug were absolutely practical creatures. The most ancient matron had decided that Miss Cummings was too old to find a husband. So she had stated the fact and given Miss Cummings the sharp and nasty instrument so Miss Cummings could take appropriate action.

Miss Cummings furiously determined to do nothing of the kind. They couldn't make her commit suicide! But if she didn't carry out the instructions—obey the signal—do whatever obedience to the head-woman's observations would be —why . . . they might do it for her!

Miss Cummings raged privately. She might have to be withdrawn from her field investigation! Another female anthropologist might have to take over! It could mean that the definitive anthropological report on the Krug race-culture would be written by somebody else, and contain merely a falsely warm acknowledgement of her contribution to the study in a preface nobody would ever read!

Miss Cummings began to wear a chip on her shoulder. It seemed to her that the villagers regarded her with mild reproof for being alive. The most authoritative matron stopped her in the street and repeated her two statements—the one that meant she was venerable without children, and the one meaning finality. A day or so later, two other matrons repeated them. A day later still, and Miss Cummings found herself ostracized. Even the Krug maidens said coldly to her that she was venerable and had no children and—finality.

It was heart-breaking, and it was more than a little frightening. But also it was enraging. Miss Cummings felt that the Krug were her project! They belonged to her! She had learned their language! She had made complete evaluations of their technology and work-habits and the gradations of social prestige and had reported fully on their marriage-customs! She would not give them up!

She took to sleeping with the tiny, almost invisible hand-weapon under her head—so far as she managed to sleep at all. But after two days in which she was ignored by all the village, she slept from pure weariness and then was awakened by the usual morning-noises from the jungle. Only this morning she found herself sitting bolt upright, and frightened.

She heard voices. Krug voices. Her heart skipped beats. Perhaps this would be violence on the way. She'd been given the signal to commit suicide and she hadn't done it. Perhaps now she was to have forcible assistance. . . .

She peered out of her doorway, ready to give an emergency-signal for rescue by helicopters from the ship. There was a great congregation of the village in the center of the maidens'-circle of huts. Krug-children raced and scampered about. The maidens of the village fairly jittered with hopeful agitation. The congress of matrons examined a *crythli* shell. As before, they examined it in the matter of near-sighted alumnae caught without their glasses. As if they were smelling it.

Then the most ancient matron, the headwoman of the village, made grunting noises to the others. She marched firmly to the hut occupied by Miss Cummings. She presented the *crythli* shell. And Miss Cummings took it.

She explained the matter crisply to her associates on the survey-ship. She would expect, she said, to be picked up shortly after nightfall. She would give a suitable warning and advance estimate of the time. But this was a perfect opportunity to record the initiatory ceremonies preceding matrimony among the Krug. It could not be expected that anybody else would have the same chance. So, once the male Krug had appeared, she would expect helicopters to drop smoke-bombs, descend in their midst guided by aerial flares, and carry her away with the absolutely invaluable anthropological treasure of a Krug bridal outfit. In the meanwhile she was, of course, armed.

The children rushed into the jungle. They returned and be-

103

gan to build a house. Miss Cummings, herself, was taken in hand by the village matrons. She had her personal communicator turned on and during all the daylight hours it transmitted scientific anthropological data which sent the staff on the survey-ship into ecstasies. Much of it is still unintelligible, and nobody but another anthropologist would find any of it interesting. But it all got down on tape. For one thing, there was more detailed data about Th'Tark than anybody had dreamed existed, and Miss Cummings' claim to be *the* authority on the Krug was settled for all time.

There was just one curious omission in the staff's and Miss Cummings' reaction. It did not occur to them that Th'Tark might have arranged their triumph, as part of the business of keeping the Krug from being exterminated.

Presently the cloudbank began to shade slightly toward a darker hue, and when it was distinctly gray Miss Cummings came out of the new kraal-type house that had been built for her prospective matronly estate. She wore the bridal costume of the village. And even Miss Cummings was almost overwhelmed by its richness. It was barbaric, of course. It was crude. But the luminous, changing colors of the pearl headdress and necklaces, and the incredible richness of the arm-bands and shell ornament gave her an extraordinary sensation.

The light faded still more, and the children disappeared, and presently the sky was black—and consequently all of the village—and then they returned, with the smallest child of all carrying a lighted torch while the others bore unlighted ones.

Miss Cummings sat in darkness, arrayed in wedding garb of a richness such as no human daughter of a sultan ever wore. There were the night-noises of the jungle. She murmured into her communicator. A reassuring voice spoke in her invisible ear-receiver. The copter rescue-party was ready. Besides, she had her small hand-weapon in case of need. She was not even faintly timid, now. The data obtained today had made her scientific reputation permanent. From now on she would be secure in the fame of being the first truly great authority on the race-culture of the Krug of the Summer Sea on Venus. With that splendor in mind, she could not be afraid. And after five weeks and more in a Krug village she could assuredly not be frightened by any mere male!

There was a single, flickering torch some fifty yards away, solicitously held by the smallest ambulatory Krug child. There was a waiting, breathless silence for a very long time.

Then a voice panted words in Kruggish speech. A matron

grunted. The child with the lighted torch passed the flame to another. The lighting spread. There were fifty flaming torches in the village night.

And Miss Cummings looked with dazed, and shocked, and wholly incredulous eyes at Ray Hale.

He was smeared with pigments to enhance the Kruglikeness of the human race. He bore a burden of *crythli* shell. He looked at her, and his eyes widened with shock. Then sweat poured out on his skin in the torchlight. He knew her not only as a human woman, but as herself—and he was the one person she unfeignedly and by long habit hated past all considerations of charity.

He swallowed, and then panted:

"Play up! Or we'll both be killed!"

Miss Cummings caught her breath. He said more shrilly:

"Play up, I tell you!"

Miss Cummings said unsteadily, with her voice a mere whisper:

"There are copters overhead. I've only to call them—"

Hale glared at her like a trapped wild beast. His desperation was so evident that Miss Cummings sensed a deep approval among the female Krug about her.

"You married my little sister," said Miss Cummings in a strange, toneless monotone. "She loved you, and you broke her heart. You beat her! You were everything that was vile to her—and she died when you left her because she loved you. I've prayed that death would strike you down! Oh, you beast-beast-beast—"

A murmur of admiration from the Krug matrons. At least, it seemed so. Hale sweated in the torchlight. He gabbled:

"They'll kill me if you don't play up! You too!"

It was a lie. Miss Cummings did not know how she knew, but she was fully aware that her behavior accorded with the ideal of Kruggish female scorn of all masculinity. The most proper of previous Krug maidens had never displayed such magnificent scorn for their bridegrooms. Miss Cummings was abstractedly aware that she would be the pattern of bridal propriety from now on.

Ray Hale put down a *crythli* shell. He trembled with his terror, but he went through the routine of matrimony among the Krug. Shell after lustrous shell, coiled, iridescent, color-changing beauty—he laid down the customary offering before Miss Cummings.

"I can let them kill you," she whispered, her throat taut. "They won't be punished. I can let them kill you as you should be killed—or I can call down the copters. . . ."

There was a voice in her ears. The rescue-party overhead was ready to swoop down, but it was bewildered. They were waiting a summons for action. They heard highly improbable human speech where nothing of the sort should be. The voice asked anxious questions. Miss Cummings recovered herself.

"Something unexpected has developed," she said in a level voice for her communicator to send aloft. "I find that I am perfectly safe. I am confident that I will not need to be rescued. But make sure that all the recorders are ready for later data."

She flipped off the communicator-switch.

In the torchlight Ray Hale looked convincingly Kruglike and desperate and despairing as he ceased the putting-down of shell and stared at Miss Cummings with the air of a man who has heard his death sentence and waits for it to be carried out. He suddenly babbled:

"Here! Pearls! I'll give you all of them! Gallons of them! Anything—anything! But don't let them kill me. . . ."

He poured a double handful of *crythli* pearls into her lap. And Miss Cummings rose. She was ashen-white, and she hated Ray Hale as she had never hated any other human being. But she was also an anthropologist. And Hale could not possibly have undertaken this enterprise if he hadn't gathered scientific information Miss Cummings still lacked.

Her lips twisted themselves into the most mirthless and seemingly most scornful of smiles. Actually, it was a grimace of anguish. She reached out and touched him—with the muzzle of her almost-invisible handweapon.

"If you try to escape in the darkness," said Miss Cummings, "I will pull the trigger when I feel no pressure on this gun."

A child dashed a torch to the ground. Instantly all the spouting flames were rolling in the earth and small Krug children were stamping on them. Miss Cummings shepherded Hale into the kraal-house that had been built that day for her.

"I think," she said thinly, "you have information I lack. I shall turn on my communicator, now, and you will tell all you know about the Krug. It will be recorded for study. Then I will decide whether to kill you or not."

She stood beside him in the darkness. He gasped. She prodded him with questions—and with the weapon.

The weapon was part of Miss Cummings' equipment. It was very small, and it fired electronically, and when the slack on the trigger was taken up it necessarily emitted microwave radiation. The fact was very useful on earth. It made the illicit use of weapons impractical, because armed officers arrived within minutes anywhere the trigger-slack of a weapon was taken up, and this worked out nicely for law-abiding citizens, but not so well for the lawless. On Venus the same fact kept non-terrestrials from making use of human weapons without permission. But for Miss Cummings, the important thing was that the emission of radiation from an electronic weapon was accompanied by a high-pitched humming sound.

Hale heard the thin drone of the pistol, and knew that Miss Cummings had only to tighten her finger ever so slightly to end his life. The sound meant that she was ready and willing to do it.

He whimpered. He was in a very great hurry to leave the bridal dwelling. He'd meant to remain there only minutes. But he did not dare to say why. When Miss Cummings asked him questions in a thinly level voice, he babbled an almost incoherent excuse for trying to go through the Krug marriage ceremony with a Krug female. But Miss Cummings wore the *crythli*-pearl headdress. She stopped him.

The thin whining sound of the ready-for-firing weapon drove him frantic, in combination with his other reasons for fear. He panted the truth. He'd made the ceremonial offering of a *crythli* shell to the center of the circle of maidens' cottages. He'd known that a bride would be chosen and a kraal-house built. The instant he entered the dwelling he meant— he panted it—to knock the female unconscious and escape with the costume worth millions of credits on earth.

"But," said Miss Cummings with the same thin steadiness, "you offered me gallons of pearls. How many times have you done this?"

He whimpered. He quivered with the need to flee. But she said as steadily and as deliberately as before:

"You would not risk only stunning the brides. You killed them, did you not? You strangled them?"

Hale babbled that the Krug were not human. It was not murder to kill them. And this was true—so far. Hale was mad to get away from the village now. Miss Cummings considered that he was fearful of a copter coming to pick him up as a criminal.

"Nobody will come from the ship unless I call them," she said with a sort of unearthly reasonableness. "It would spoil my research project for a copter to land in the village. But my sister died because she loved you. If you wish to live, you will tell me . . ."

What followed was one of the most peculiar data-gathering interviews in the history of anthropology. With his own reasons for desperate and headlong flight urging him, and the whine of the taut-triggered weapon holding him still, Hale tried—stumbling over his words in his haste—to answer all Miss Cummings chose to ask. He did not even try to lie. He gabbled in his effort to satisfy her scientific curiosity in the shortest possible time. He trembled. He shook. Presently his breathing was only gasps. But she was inexorable. She held consultations with the ship to clarify what other questions she should ask. She reflected, and phrased her questions with precision. And all the time the weapon whined softly, ready to destroy Hale if he tried to flee.

It was an excellent interview, though. Miss Cummings got a full picture of the male side of the marriage-custom story, which no trader had been able to do. Male Krug were despised. But to marry they had to gather *crythli* shells. Preferably those bearing pearls. Tending to grow incoherent in his haste, Hale told her where the *crythli* shells were found and how they had to be acquired. Only a Krug would do it, and a Krug wouldn't do it for money. It had to be the stark necessity which drove a Krug to marriage. . . .

"I've got to get away from here!" panted Hale shrilly. "I can't stay here! I can't—I can't—"

Miss Cummings said thinly:

"I shall remain in the village a few days more to gather the data needed to complete what I know now. It would be inconvenient to have your body here. So I do not kill you. Go!"

She drew back the muzzle of the weapon, but it still whined faintly. She was aware of exhaustion, now. She'd remained standing and terribly tense for a length of time she didn't realize. Actually it was to be measured in hours. Only an anthropologist could have done it, and only then to gather information there would be no second chance to procure. Miss Cummings felt herself wilting as Hale sprang away from her and dived desperately into the blackness outside the kraal-house door.

But, weary as she was, she burst incontinently into sobs. She had been very, very fond of the sister whom Hale had married fifteen years before and who had died of her love for him. Miss Cummings wept exhaustedly. She was too exhausted even to try to muffle her sobbing.

But this, as it happened, was considered suitable behavior in a new matron. Among the Krug a new-wedded bride weeps loudly when her brand new husband makes his way back into the darkness from which he came. It is, in a way, a signal of his departure. Also, it covers any sounds that may be made outside.

As in this case.

When Miss Cummings appeared in public, next morning, she was saluted with the honorific pronouns she rated as a married lady Krug. She was regarded with complete approval, and in a matter of four days moɪe she had gathered absolutely all the information the Krug female language could convey in the absence of a word for *why*. She felt only one minor disappointment as an anthropologist. It was that she did not take part in the making of the mound-like flower-bed she found before her kraal-house in the morning, nor in its decoration with the *crythli* shell that Hale had set out in the torchlight. Even the flowers were planted for her. But she watered them dutifully.

Before the week was out she went back to the ship, to the stark amazement of the Krug. In time she wrote a book about the Krug culture which brought her eminence among anthropologists and is still the standard work. Incidentally, her book prevented the extermination of the Krug by revealing where the *crythli* mollusks grow and how they have to be obtained. Humans do not attempt to gather them. They still leave that to the Krug. But it is now the custom to purchase the decorative shells from Krug villages when a kraal-house is torn down because of the demise of the lady Krug who lived in it. Then the *crythli* shells have no more significance to the Krug, and they part with them readily for a fair price in quinine. Which, of course, means that the supply of *crythli* shell is steady but moderate and the price remains stable—which is good for interplanetary trade. Sometimes a few pearls are purchased, too.

And this may possibly have been the reason for the whole affair. Th'Tark could have arranged it. If there is a Th'Tark, this could be the explanation. But one has doubts.

The most recent editions of Miss Cummings' book have a three-page appendix added to them. The three pages add little of importance to the anthropological side of her work, but they do complete the biology. They report recent discoveries that once a Krug maiden becomes a matron, she produces offspring with a fine regularity for all the rest of her life, though she never sees her husband again. Biologists tend to speak of Krug males as "drones," nowadays, by analogy with honeybees and ants, whose males like the Krug are driven from the communities of working females, and who die after their mating. And philologists put a word in, too, arguing that since the Krug language is incapable of expressing the operations of logic, there is no evidence that the Krug think in concepts —i.e., that they are reasoning beings. And the biologists join in zestfully to point out that the Krug technology and symbiosis with vegetation is certainly no more complex than that of the leaf-cutter ants. Other myrmidae and some kinds of bees and wasps approach it, too. Altogether, they make out quite a case.

The anthropologists consider that they have the last word, though. They point out triumphantly that the Krug must be considered human because there is no other case, among irrational animals, of social participation in a marriage rite. And especially, they point out, no other non-human creature engages in any sort of funerary activity. But the Krug do have a marriage ceremony. It is elaborate. They have a socially recognized honeymoon, during which the bride and her new husband are alone in the new home built for the bride, and during which for a matter of hours every other Krug returns to her own dwelling and the privacy of the wedding pair is absolute. Even the end of the honeymoon is no less officially recognized, because after a fixed interval—of as much as four hours—the Krug matrons gather about the hut again. When the new Krug bridegroom flees his new wife's hut he is met by this committee of mated females. And they dispatch him very dexterously with a sharp wooden instrument and bury him in a neat mound before his widow's door and ornament the mound with *crythli* shells. And afterward his widow dutifully waters the flowers that are planted there.

This, the anthropologists say, is human behavior.

It is not settled yet. Maybe Hale could throw some light upon the question. He knew a great deal about the Krug. Even in his frantic haste to tell all he knew, it took hours for Miss Cummings to exhaust her list of questions and the secondary questions suggested by his replies. Maybe he did know more than she learned from him, because she couldn't but be affected by his frantic anxiety to be gone. But nobody knows how much Hale had found out. He has never been seen since his Krug-wedding night, on Venus or elsewhere.

Maybe the only way to find out the facts would be to ask Th'Tark, who could, just possibly, have arranged the whole affair. It prevented the extermination of the Krug by the march of progress. Th'Tark would have wanted to bring that about, certainly.

If there is or was a Th'Tark.

The Skit-tree Planet

THE COMMUNICATOR-PHONE set up a clamor when the sky was just beginning to gray in what, on this as yet unnamed planet, they called the east because the local sun rose there. The call-wave had turned on the set and Wentworth kicked off his blankets and stumbled from his bunk in the atmosphere-flier, and went sleepily forward to answer. He pushed the answer-stud and said wearily:

"Hello! What's the trouble? . . . Talk louder, there's some static . . . Oh . . . No, there's no trouble. Why should there be? . . . The devil I'm late reporting! Haynes and I obeyed orders and tried to find the end of a confounded skit-tree plantation. We chased our tails all day long, but we made so much westing that we gained a couple of hours light. So it isn't sunrise yet, where we are. . . ." He yawned. "Oh, we set down the flier on a sort of dam and went to sleep. . . . No, nothing happened. We're used to feeling creepy. We thrive on it. Haynes says he's going to do a sculpture group of a skit-tree planter which will be just an eye peeking around a tree-trunk. . . . No! Dammit, no! We photographed a couple of hundred thousand square miles of skit-trees growing in neat rows, and we photographed dams, and canals, and a whole irrigation system, but not a sign of a living creature . . . No cities, no houses, no ruins, no nothing. . . . I've got a theory, McRae, about what happened to the skit-tree planters." He yawned again. "Yeah. I think they built up a magnificent civilization and then found a snark. . . . Snark! S-N-A-R-K. . . . Yes. And the snark was a boojum." He paused. "So they silently faded away."

He grinned at the profanity that came out of the communicator-speaker. Then McRae cut off, back at the irreverently nicknamed *Galloping Cow* which was the base ship of the Extra-Solarian Research Institute expedition to this star-cluster. Wentworth stretched, and looked out of the atmosphere-flier's windows. He absently noticed that the static on the communication-set kept up, which was rather odd on a FM receiver. But before the fact could have any meaning, he saw something in motion in the pale gray light of dawn. He squinted. Then he caught his breath.

He stood frozen until the moving object vanished. It moved, somehow, as if it carried something. But it was bigger than the *Galloping Cow!* Only after it vanished did he breathe again, and then he licked his lips and blinked.

Haynes' voice came sleepily from the bunk-space of the flier.

"What's from the *Galloping Cow?* Planning to push off for Earth?"

Wentworth took a deep breath and stared where the moving thing had gone out of sight. Then he said very quietly:

"No. . . . McRae was worried because we hadn't reported. It's two hours after sunrise back where the ship is." He swallowed. "Want to get up now?"

"I could do with coffee," said Haynes, "pending a start for home."

Wentworth heard him drop his feet to the floor. And Wentworth pinched himself and winced, and swallowed again, and then twisted the opener of a beverage can labeled *"Coffee"* and it began to make bubbling noises. He put it aside to heat and brew itself, and pulled out two breakfast-rations. He put them in the readier. Then he stared again out the flier's window.

The light outside grew stronger. To the north—if where the sun rose was east—a low but steep range of mountains began just beyond the spot where the flier had landed for the night. It had settled down on a patently artificial embankment of earth, some fifty feet high, that ran out toward the skit-tree sea from one of the lower mountain spurs. The moving thing had gone into those mountains, as if it carried something. But it was bigger.

Haynes came forward, yawning.

"I feel," he said, and yawned again, "as if this were going to be a good day. I wish I had some clay to mess with. I might even do a portrait bust of you, Wentworth, lacking a prettier model."

"Keep an eye out the window," said Wentworth, "and meanwhile you might set the table."

He went back to his bunk and dressed quickly. His expression was blank and incredulous. Again, once, he pinched himself. But he was awake. He went back to where steaming coffee and the breakfast-platters waited on the board normally used for navigation.

The communication-set still emitted static—curiously steady, scratchy noise that should not have come in on a frequency-modulation set at all, and especially should not have come in on a planet which had plainly once been

112

inhabited, but whose every inhabitant and every artifact had vanished utterly. Habitation was so evident, and seemed to have been so recent, that most of the members of the expedition felt a creepy sensation as if eyes were watching them all the time. But that was absurd, of course.

Haynes ate his chilled fruit. The readier had thawed the frozen fruit, and not only thawed but cooked the rest of breakfast. Wentworth drank a preliminary cup of coffee.

"I've just had an unsettling experience, Haynes," he said carefully. "Do I look unusually cracked, to you?"

"Not for you," said Haynes. "Not even for any man who not only isn't married but isn't even engaged. I attribute my splendid mental health to the fact that I'm going to get married as soon as we get back to Earth. —Have I mentioned it before?"

Wentworth ignored the question.

"Something's turned up—with a reason back of it," he said in a queer tone. "Check me on this. We found the first skit-trees on Cetis Alpha Three. They grew in neat rows that stretched out for miles and miles. They had patently been planted by somebody who knew what he was doing, and why. We found dams, and canals, and a complete irrigation system. We found places where ground had been terraced and graded, and where various trees and plants grew in what looked like a cockeyed form of decorative planting. Those clearings could have been sites for cities, only there were no houses or ruins, or any sign that anything had ever been built there. We hunted that planet with a fine-toothed comb, and we'd every reason to believe it had recently been inhabited by a highly civilized race—but we never found so much as a chipped rock or a brick or any shaped piece of metal or stone to prove it. A civilization had existed, and it had vanished, and when it vanished it took away everything it had worked with—except that it didn't tear up its plantings or put back the dirt it had moved. Right?"

"Put dispassionately," said Haynes cheerfully, "you sound like you're crazy. But you're stating facts. Okay so far."

"McRae tore his hair," Wentworth went on, "because he couldn't take back anything but photographs. —Oh, you did a very fine sculpture of a skit-tree fruit, but we froze some real ones for samples, anyhow. We went on to another solar system. And on a planet there we found skit-trees planted in neat rows reaching for miles and miles, and dams, and canals, and cleared places—and nothing else. McRae frothed at the mouth with frustration. Some non-human race had space-travel. Eh?"

Haynes took a cup of coffee.

"The inference," he agreed, "was made unanimously by all the personnel of the *Galloping Cow*."

Wentworth glanced nervously out the flier window.

"We kept on going. On nine planets in seven solar systems we found skit-tree plantations with rows up to six and seven hundred miles long—following great-circle courses, by the way—and dams and irrigation systems. Whoever planted those skit-trees had space-travel on an interstellar scale, because the two farthest of the planets were two hundred light-years apart. But we've never found a single artifact of the race that planted the skit-trees."

"True," said Haynes. "Too true! If we'd loaded up the ship with souvenirs of the first non-human civilized race ever to be discovered, we'd have headed for home and I'd be a married man now."

Wentworth said painfully;

"Listen! Could it be that we never found any artifacts because there weren't any? Could it be that a creature—a monstrous creature—could have developed instincts that led it to make dams and canals like beavers do, and plantings like some kinds of ants do, only with the sort of geometric precision that is characteristic of a spider's web? Could we have misread mere specialized instinct as intelligence?"

Haynes blinked.

"Could be— No. Seven solar systems. Two hundred light-years. A specific species, obviously originating on only one planet, spread out over two hundred light-years. Not unless your animal could do space-travel and carry skit-tree seeds with him. —What gave you that idea?"

"I saw something," said Wentworth. He took another deep breath. "I'm not going to tell you what it was like, I don't really believe it myself. And I am scared green! But I wanted to clear that way before I mentioned—this. Listen!"

He waved his hand at the communicator-set. Static came out of its speaker in a clacking, monotonous, but continuous turned-down din.

Haynes listened.

"What the—? We shouldn't get that kind of stuff on a frequency-modulation set!"

"We shouldn't. Something's making it. Maybe what I saw was—domesticated. In any case, I'm going to go out and look for its tracks where I saw it moving."

"You? Not we? What's the matter with both of us?"

Wentworth shook his head.

"I'll take a flame-pistol—though running-shoes would be more practical. You can hover overhead, if you like. But don't try to be heroic, Haynes!"

Haynes whistled.

"How about air reconnaissance first?" he demanded. "We can look for tracks with a telescope. If we see a jabberwock or something on that order, we can skip for the blue. If we don't find anything from the air, all right. But a preliminary scout from aloft!"

Wentworth licked his lips.

"That might be sensible," he admitted, "but the damned thing scared me so that I've got to face it sooner or later. All right. Clear away this stuff and I'll take the ship up."

While Haynes slid the cups and platters into the refuse-disposal unit, he seated himself in the pilot's seat, turned off the watch-dog circuit that would have waked them if anything living had come within a hundred yards of the flier during the night-time, and gave the jets a warming-up flow of fuel. Thirty seconds later the flier lifted smoothly and leveled off to hover at four hundred feet. Wentworth took bearings on their landing-place. There were no other landmarks that would serve, for keeping the flier stationary.

The skit-trees began where the ground grew fairly level, and they went on beyond the horizon. They were clumps of thin and brittle stalks which rose straight up for eighty feet and then branched out and bore copious quantities of a fruit for which no human being could imagine any possible use. Each clump of trees was a geometrically perfect circle sixty feet in diameter. There was always just ninety-two feet between clumps. They reached out in rows far beyond the limit of vision. Only the day before, the flier had covered fifteen hundred miles of westing without coming to the end of this particular planting.

With the flier hovering, Wentworth used a high-power telescope to search below. He hunted for long, long minutes, examining minutely every square foot of half a dozen between-clump aisles without result. There was no sign of the passage of any creature, much less of the apparition he would much rather not believe in.

"I think," he said reluctantly, "I'm going to have to go down and hunt on foot. Maybe there wasn't anything. Maybe I'm crazy."

Haynes said mildly:

"Speaking of craziness, is or isn't that city yonder a delusion?"

115

He pointed, and Wentworth jerked about. Many, many miles away, something reared upward beyond the horizon. It was indubitably a city—and they had searched nine planets over without finding a single scrap of chipped stone to prove the reality of the skit-tree planters. Wentworth could see separate pinnacles and what looked like skyways connecting them far above-ground. He snapped his camera to his binoculars and focussed them—and of course the camera with them. He saw architectural details of bewildering complexity. He snapped the shutter of his camera.

"That," said Wentworth, "gets top priority. There's no doubt about this!"

The thing he had seen before sunrise was so completely incredible that it was easier to question his vision than to believe in it. He flung over the jet-controls so that the drive-jets took the fuel from the supporting ones. The flier went roaring toward the far-away city.

"Take over," he told Haynes. "I'm going to call McRae back. He'll break down and cry with joy."

He pushed the call-button. Seconds later a voice came out of the communicator, muffled and made indistinct by the roar of the jets. Wentworth reported. He turned a tiny television scanner on the huge, lacy construction rising from a site still beyond the horizon. McRae's shout of satisfaction was louder than the jets. He bellowed and cut off instantly.

"The *Galloping Cow*," said Wentworth, "is shoving off. McRae's giving this position and telling all mapping-parties to make for it. And he'll climb out of atmosphere to get here fast. He wants to see that city!"

The flier wabbled, as Haynes' hands on the controls wabbled.

"What city?" he asked in an odd voice.

Wentworth stared unbelievingly. There was nothing in sight but the lunatic rows of skit-trees, stretching out with absolutely mechanical exactitude to the limit of vision on the right, on the left, ahead, and behind to the very base of the mountains. There simply wasn't any city. Wentworth gaped.

"Pull that film out of the camera. Take a look at it. Were we seeing things?"

Haynes pulled out the already-developed film. The city showed plainly. It had gone on television to the *Galloping Cow*, too. It had not been an illusion. Wentworth pushed the call-button again as the flier went on toward a vanished destination. After a moment he swore.

"McRae lost no time! He's out of air already, and our set won't reach him. —Where'd that city go?"

He set the supersonic collision-alarm in action. The radar. They revealed nothing. The city simply no longer existed.

They searched incredulously for twenty minutes, at four hundred miles an hour. The radar picked up nothing. The collision-alarm picked up no echoes.

"It was here!" growled Wentworth. "We'll go back and start over!"

He sent the flier hurtling back toward the hills and the embankment where it had rested during the night. The communicator rasped a sudden furious burst of static. Wentworth, for no reason whatever, jerked his eyes behind. The city was there again.

Haynes photographed it feverishly as the flier banked and whirled back toward it. For a full minute it was in plain view, and the static was loud. Then the static cut off. Simultaneously, the city vanished once more.

Again a crazy circling. But the utterly monotonous landscape below showed no sign of a city-site, and it was impossible to be sure that the flier actually quartered the ground below, or whether it circled over the same spot again and again, or what.

"If McRae turns up in the *Galloping Cow*," said Haynes, "and doesn't find a damned thing, maybe he'll think we've all gone crazy and had better go home. And then—"

"Then you'll get married!" said Wentworth savagely. "Skip it! I've got an idea! Back to the mountains once more. . . ."

The flier whirled yet again and sped back toward its night's resting-place. Ten miles from it, and five thousand feet up, the static began still again. Wentworth kicked a smoke-bomb release and whirled the flier about so sharply that his head snapped forward from the sudden centrifugal force. There was the city. The flier roared straight for it. Static rattled out of the communicator. One minute. Two. He kicked the smoke-bomb release again. Already the first bomb had hit ground and ignited. A billowing mass of smoke welled up from its position. The second reached ground and made a second smoke-signal. Ten miles on, he dropped a third. The smoke-signals would burn for an hour, and gave him a perfect line on the vanishing city. This time it did not vanish. It grew larger and larger, and details appeared, and more details . . .

It was a unit; a design of infinite complexity, but so perfectly integrated that it was a single design. Storey upon

117

storey, with far-flung skyways connecting its turrets, it was a vision of completely alien beauty. It rose ten thousand feet from the skit-trees about its base. Its base was two miles square.

"They built high," said Wentworth grimly, "so they wouldn't use any extra ground they could plant their damned skit-trees on. —I'm going to land short of it, Haynes."

The vertical jets took over smoothly as he cut the drive. The flier slowed, and two blasts forward stopped it dead, and then it descended smoothly. Wentworth had checked not more than a hundred yards from the outermost tower. It appeared to be made of completely seamless metal, incised with intricate decorative designs. Which was incredible. But the most impossible thing of all was that there was no movement anywhere. No stirring. No shifting. Not even furtive twinklings as of eyes peering from the strangely-shaped window-openings. And when the flier landed gently between two circular clumps of skit-trees and Wentworth cut off the jets and then turned off even the communicator—then there was silence.

The silence was absolute. Two miles high, there towered a city which could house millions of people. And it was utterly without noise and utterly without motion in any part.

"And then the prince went into the castle," said Wentworth savagely, "and he kissed the Sleeping Beauty on the lips, and she opened her eyes with a glad little cry, and they were married and lived happily ever after. Coming, Haynes?"

"I'll come," said Haynes. "But I don't kiss anybody. I'm engaged!"

Wentworth got out of the flier. Never yet had they found a single dangerous animal on any of the nine planets on which skit-trees grew—barring whatever it was he had seen that morning. Whoever planted skit-trees wiped out dangerous fauna. That had been one of the few seeming certainties. But all the same, Wentworth put a flame-pistol in his belt before he started for the city.

And then he stopped short. There was a flickering. The city was blotted out. A blank metal wall stood before him. It reared all around the flier and the men in it. Between them and the city. Shining, seamless, gleaming metal, perfectly circular and a hundred feet high. It neatly enclosed a circle two hundred yards across, and hence some clumps of skit-trees with the men.

"Now—where the hell did that come from?" panted Wentworth.

118

Then, abruptly, everything went black. There was darkness. Absolute, opaque, blinding night.

For perhaps two seconds it was unbroken. Then Haynes, still in the flier, pushed the button that turned on the emergency landing-lights. Twin beams of some hundreds of thousands candlepower lashed out, and recoiled from polished metal, and spread about and were reflected and re-reflected. There was a metal roof atop the circular metal wall. Men and flier and clumps of skit-trees were sealed up in a monstrous metal cylinder.

Wentworth swore. Then he cried furiously;

"It isn't so! It simply can't be so!"

He marched angrily to the nearest of the metal walls. Twin shadows of his figure were cast on before him by the landing-light beams. Weird reflections of the shadows and the lights—distorted crazily by the polished surface—appeared on every hand.

He reached the metal wall. He pulled out his flame-pistol and tapped at it. The wall was solid. He backed off five paces and sent a flame-pistol beam at it. The flame splashed from the metal in a coruscating shower. But nothing happened. Absolutely nothing. When he turned off the pistol the metal was utterly unmarred. It was not even red-hot.

Haynes said absurdly;

"The sleeping beauty woke up, Wentworth. —What's the matter?"

He saw Wentworth gazing with stupefaction at a place where the metal cylinder touched ground. There was the beginning of a circular clump of skit-trees. And he saw a stalk at a slight angle. It came out of the metal wall. The skit-trees were in the wall. They came out of it. He saw another that went into it.

He went back to the flier and climbed in. He turned the communicator up to maximum power. The racket that came out of it was deafening. He punched the call-button. Again and again and again. Nothing happened. He turned the set off.

The dead stillness which followed was daunting.

"Well?" said Haynes.

"It's impossible," said Wentworth, "but I can explain everything. That wall isn't real."

"Then we ram through it?"

"We'd kill ourselves!" Wentworth told him exasperatedly. "It's solid!"

"Not real, but solid?" asked Haynes. "A bit unusual, that. When I get back to Earth and am a happily married man,

119

I'll try to have a more plausible story than that to tell my wife if I ever come home late—not that I ever will."

Wentworth looked at him. And Haynes grinned. But there was sweat on his face. Wentworth grunted.

"I'm scared too," he said sourly, "but I don't make bad jokes to cover up. This can be licked. It's got to be!"

"What is it?"

"How do I know?" demanded Wentworth. "It makes sense, though. A city that vanishes and re-appears—apparently without anybody in it. That doesn't happen. This can—this tank we're in. There wasn't any machinery around to put up a wall like this. And the top wasn't heaved into place. It wasn't lowered down to seal us in. It didn't slide into position. One instant it wasn't there, and the next instant it was. Like something that—hm—had materialized out of nowhere. —Maybe that's it! And the city was the same sort of trick! —Maybe that's the secret of this whole civilization we're trying to trace!"

His voice echoed weirdly against the metal ceiling on every hand.

"What's the secret?"

"Materializing things! Making a—synthetic sort of matter! Making—well—force-fields that look and act like substance. Of course! If you can generate a building, why build one? We can make a magnetic field with a coil of wire and an electric current. It's just as real as a brick. It's simply different. We can make a picture on a screen. It's just as real as a painting. It's just different. Suppose we could make something like a magnetic field, with shape and coloring *and* solidity! Why not solidity? Given the trick, it should be as easy as shape or color! . . . If we had a trick like that and wanted to stop some visitors from outer space, we'd simply make the solid image of a can around them! It would be made with energy, and all the energy applied to it would flow to any threatened spot. It would draw power to fight any stress that tried to destroy it. Of course! And why should we build cities? We'd clear a place for them and generate them and maintain them simply by supplying the power needed to keep them in being! We'd make force-fields in the shape of machines, to dig canals or pile up dams. . . ."

He had raised his voice as he spoke. The solid walls and roof made echoes which clanged. He stopped short. Haynes said calmly;

"Then there wouldn't be any artifacts. When a city was abandoned, it would be wiped out as completely as the pic-

120

ture on a theatre-screen when the play is done with. But—
Wentworth—"

"Eh?"

"If we had that trick, and we'd captured some meddle-some strangers from outer space by clapping a can over them, what would we do?" He paused. "In other words, what comes next for us?"

Wentworth clamped his teeth together.

"Get in the pilot's seat," he commanded, "and put your finger on the vertical flight button. When you see light, stab it down so we'll shoot straight up! If we trapped somebody, and if we lifted it, we'd have something worse than a trap to take care of them with. They'd do the same—and they've got what it should take!"

Silence. Haynes' voice:

"Such as?"

"I saw one Thing this morning," said Wentworth grimly. "I don't like to think about it. If they're bringing it over to snap us up when this can is lifted off of us. . . . You keep your finger on the flight-button! That Thing was bigger than the *Galloping Cow!* —I'll try to tip McRae what's happened."

He settled down by the communicator. Every ten minutes he tried to call the expedition's ship. Every time there came a monstrous roar of static as the set came on, and no other sound at all. Aside from that, nothing happened. Absolutely nothing. The flier lay on the ground with an unnatural as-sortment of reflected and re-reflected light-beams from the twin landing-lamps. There were four clumps of skit-trees sharing the prison with the flier and the men.

Silence. Stillness. Nothing . . . Every ten minutes Went-worth called the *Galloping Cow.*

It was an hour and a half before there came an answering when Wentworth made his call.

". . *llo!*" came McRae's voice through the crackling stat-ic. "*Down in . . . gain . . . no sign . . . sort anywhere . . .*"

"Get a directional on me!" snapped Wentworth. "Can you hear me above the static?"

"*What stat . . . oice perfectly clear. . . .*" came McRae's booming. "Keep . . . talking. . . ."

Wentworth blinked. No static at the *Galloping Cow!* When his ears were practically deafened? Then it made sense. All of it!

"I'll keep talking," he said fervently. "Use the directional and locate me. But don't try to help me direct. Take a bearing from where you find me to where a fifty-foot dirt

121

embankment sticks out from a mountain-spur to the north. Get on that line and you'll hear the static, all right! It's in a beam coming right here at me! Follow that static back to the mountains, and when you find where it's being projected from, you'll find some skit-tree planters with all the artifacts your little heart desires! Only maybe you'll have to blast them . . ."

He swallowed.

"It works out to sense," he went on more calmly. "They built up a civilization based on generating instead of building the things they wanted to use. Our force-fields are globular, because the generator's inside. If you want a force-field to have a definite shape, you have to generate it differently. Their cities and their machines weren't substance, though they were solid enough. They were force-fields! The generators were off at a distance, throwing the force-field they wanted where they needed it. They projected solidities like we project pictures on a screen. They projected their cities. Their tools. Probably their spaceships too! That's why we never found artifacts! We looked where installations had been, instead of where they were generated and flung to the spot where they were wanted. There's a beam full of static coming from those mountains—"

Light! With all the blinding suddenness of an atomic explosion, there was light. Wentworth had a moment's awareness of sunshine on the brittle stalks of skit-trees, and then of upward acceleration so fierce that it was like a blow. The atmosphere-flier hurtled skyward with all its lift-jets firing full blast—and there was the *Galloping Cow* lumbering ungracefully through atmosphere at ten thousand feet, some twelve or more miles away.

And McRae's voice came out of a communicator which now picked up no static whatever.

"What the devil?" he boomed. "We saw something that looked like a big metal tank, and it vanished and you went skyward from where it'd been like a bat out of hell—"

"Suppose you follow me," said Wentworth grimly. "The skit-tree planters on this planet, anyhow, don't want us around. By pure accident, I got a line on where they were. They lured me away from their place by projecting a city. I went to look—and it vanished. I played hide and seek with it until they changed tactics and let it stay in existence. Maybe they thought we'd land on it, high up, and get out of the flier to explore. Then the city'd have vanished and we'd have dropped a mile or two—hard. But we landed on the ground instead, and they clapped a jail around us. I don't know what they intended, but you came along and they let the jail vanish to keep you from examining it. And now we'll go talk to them!"

The flier was streaking vengefully back to the embankment to where only that morning, before sunrise, Wentworth had seen something he still didn't like to think about. The *Galloping Cow* veered around to follow, with all the elephantine grace of the animal for which she had been unofficially christened. She'd been an Earth-Pluto freighter before conversion for this expedition, and she was a staunch vessel, but not a handy one.

The flier dived for the hills. Wentworth's jaws were hard and angry. The *Galloping Cow* trailed, wallowing. The flier quartered back and forth across the hills, examining every square inch of ground. . . .

Nothing. Absolutely nothing. The search went on. The communicator boomed McRae's voice:

"They're playing possum. We'll land and make a camp and prepare to hunt on foot."

Wentworth growled angrily. He continued to search. Deeper and deeper into the hills. Going over and over every bit of terrain. Then, quite suddenly, the communicator emitted babbling sounds. Shoutings. Incoherent outcries. From the ship, of course. There were sudden, whining crashes—electronic cannon going off at a panic-stricken rate. Then a ghastly crashing sound—and silence.

The flier zoomed until Haynes and Wentworth could see. They paled. Wentworth uttered a raging cry.

The *Galloping Cow* had landed. Her ports were open and men had emerged. But now a Thing had attacked the ship with a ruthless, irresistible ferocity. It was bigger than the *Galloping Cow*. It stood a hundred feet high at the shoulder. It was armored and possessed of prodigious jaws and incredible teeth. It was all the nightmares of mechanistic minds rolled into one and then magnified. It must have materialized from nothingness, because nothing so huge could have escaped Wentworth's search. But as Wentworth first looked at it the incredible jaws closed on the ship's frame and bit through the tough plates of beryllium steel as if they had been paper. It tore them away and flung them aside. A mainframe girder offered resistance. With an irresistible jerk, the Thing tore it free. And then it put its claws into the very vitals of the *Galloping Cow* and began to tear the old spaceship apart.

The crewmen spilled out and fled. The Thing snapped at one as he went by, but returned to its unbelievable destruc-

123

tion. Someone heaved a bomb into its very jaws, and it exploded—and the Thing seemed not to notice it.

Wentworth seized the controls of the flier from Haynes. He dived—not for the ship, but for the space between the ship and the mountains. He flung the small craft into crazy, careening gyrations in that space.

And then the communicator shrieked with clacking static. The flier passed through the beam, but Wentworth flung it back in. He plunged toward the mountains. He lost the beam, and found it again, and lost it, and found it . . ."

"There!" he said, choking with rage. "Down from the top of that cliff! There's a hole! A cave-mouth! The beam's coming from there!"

He plunged the flier for the opening, and braked with monstrous jettings that sent rocket-fumes blindingly and chokingly into the tunnel. The flier hit—and Wentworth scrambled to the forepart of the little ship and leaped to the cliff-opening against which it bumped, and then ran into the opening, his flame-pistol flaring before him.

There was a blinding flash inside. The blue-white flame of a short-circuit making a gigantic arc. It died. The place was full of smoke, and something small ran feebly across the small space that Wentworth could see, and fell, and kicked feebly, and was still. A machine came to a jolting stop. And Wentworth, crouching fiercely, waited for more antagonists.

None came. The fumes drifted out the cave-mouth. Then he saw that the thing on the floor was a weirdly constructed space-suit, and that the thing in it was not human and looked very tired. It was dead. Then he saw an almost typical tight-beam projector, linked with heavy cables to a scanning device. He saw a model—all of five feet high—of the city he and Haynes had tried to reach. The model was of unbelievable delicacy and perfection. But the scanning system now was focused on a metal object which was a miniature Thing with claws and jaws and armor. . . . It was two feet long, and there was a cable control by which its movements could be directed. A solidity which was controlled by that ingenious mechanical toy could dig canals, or gather the crop from the tops of skit-trees—when enlarged in the projection to stand a hundred feet high at the shoulder—or it could tear apart a space-ship as a terrier rends a rat. . . .

There was more. Much more. But there was only the one small Inhabitant, who wore a space-suit on his own planet. And he was dead.

Haynes called from the flier at the cave-mouth:

124

"Wentworth! What's happened? Are you alive? What's up?" Wentworth went savagely out. He wanted to see how the *Galloping Cow* had withstood the attack. What he had seen last looked bad.

It was bad. The *Galloping Cow* was a carcass. Her engines were not too badly smashed, but her outer shell was scrap-iron, her frame was twisted wreckage, and there was no faintest hope that they could repair her in the field.

"And—I'm engaged to be married when we get back," said Haynes, white-faced. "We'll never get back in that. . . ."

Less than a month later, though, the *Galloping Cow* did head for home. Haynes, unwittingly, had made it possible. Examination of the solidity-projector revealed its principles, and Haynes—trying forlornly to make a joke—suggested that he model a statuette of the last Inhabitant to be projected a mile or two high above the skit-tree plantations now forever useless. But he was commissioned to model something else entirely, and in his exuberance his fancy wandered afar. But McRae dourly permitted the model to stand, because he was in a hurry to start.

So that, some six weeks from the morning when Wentworth saw an impossible Thing moving in the gray dawn-light on an unnamed planet, the *Galloping Cow* was almost back in touch with humanity. Two weeks more, and the outposts of civilization on Rigel would be reached. A long, skeleton tower had been built out from the old ship's battered remnant. A scanner scanned, and a beam-type projector projected the image of Haynes' making to form a solid envelope of force-field about the ship. It was much larger than the original hull had been, there would be room and to spare on the voyage home. And Haynes was utterly happy.

"Think!" he said blissfully, in the scanning-room where the force-field envelope was maintained about the ship. "Two weeks and Rigel! Two months and home! Two months and one day and I'm a married man!"

Wentworth looked at the small moving object on which the scanners focussed.

"You're a queer egg, Haynes," he said. "I don't believe you ever had a solemn thought in your head. —Do you know what wiped out those people?"

"A boojum?" asked Haynes mildly. "Tell me."

"The biologists figured it out," said Haynes. "A plague. The last poor devil wore a space-suit to keep the germs out. It seems that some wrecked Earth-ship drifted out to where one of their explorers found it. And they hauled it to ground.

125

They learned a lot, but there were germs on board they weren't used to. Coryza, for instance. In their bodies it had an incubation period of about six months, and was highly contagious all the time. Then it turned lethal. They didn't know about it in time to establish quarantines. —No wonder the poor devil wanted to kill us! We'd wiped out his race!"

"Too bad!" said Haynes. But he looked down at the small moving thing he had modeled for a new hull for the *Galloping Cow.* "You know," he said blithely, "I like this model! I may not be the best sculptor in the world—as an amateur I wouldn't expect it. But for a while after we land on earth I'm surely going to be the most famous!"

And he beamed at the jerkily moving object which was the model for the hull of the *Galloping Cow.* It was twelve hundred feet long, as it was projected about the old ship's engine-room and remaining portions. It had a stiffly extended tail and an outstretched neck and curved horns. Its legs extended and kicked, and extended and kicked.

The *Galloping Cow,* in fact, exactly fitted her name by her outward appearance, as she galloped steadily earthward through emptiness.

Thing from the Sky

MAYBE THE THING from the sky landed where it did because rain had fallen in Seco Valley for the second recorded time in sixty years. Or maybe that was only coincidence. The rainfall did bring Steve Hansun to the valley, though he hardly expected to find anything but sun-scorched rock and sun-baked sand and such impossible desert conditions that even lizards and rattlesnakes would stay away from it. Seco is Spanish for dry, and Seco Valley is hell on earth. Even Death Valley—forty miles away—is a place of lush vegetation and flowing fountains by comparison. But there had been a rainfall in Seco Valley, and for hours the parched, dust-caked rocks showed many colors and the sand drank greedily of pelting raindrops. For a space there was a steaming mist over the driest place on earth. Maybe the thing from the sky was drawn by it.

Maybe.

Steve Hansun heard about the rain after it happened. He

was Research Assistant in the Arid-Area Plants Section of a college which shall be nameless. He was working on a possible variation of the prickly pear—it was to be without prickles—which could thrive in desert regions and serve as cattle-food without each pod having to have its spines seared off with a gasoline torch. He knew Death Valley, and Seco Valley too, and he'd made a bargain with a hard-rock miner named Brady who stubbornly worked a claim some ten miles north from Seco Valley and seven thousand feet higher above sea-level.

So. . . . On a certain day the hard-rock man, Brady, saw clouds banking up all over the area of which Seco Valley was a part. It was freakish. Presently there was a parting of the clouds and Brady could see that rain was falling. Death Valley has rain—a good rain—as often as once in ten years. Naturalists and biologists gloat over the plants which spring up instantly after it and bloom for a couple of weeks before they shrivel and go back to dust in Death Valley's normal desiccation. But nobody had ever seen plants in Seco Valley. It never rains there. So Brady made amazedly sure that it was raining, and then headed across the mountains to keep the terms of his bargain with Steve.

That was one day—Wednesday. He sent a telegram to Steve about the rain and got an answer as fast as the wires could bring it. Steve was on the way. That was Thursday. Brady hung around the town of San Felice waiting for Steve's arrival. That was Friday. Friday night the thing from the sky arrived.

It wasn't a thing that could fly, itself, though something that could fly must have been involved in its arrival. It appeared over Seco Valley by night, dangling from a slender thread which reached up through a cloud-bank, and up through the stratosphere, and on up past the tropopause, and nobody can guess how many miles beyond that. The thread was very remarkable. It wasn't more than a quarter of an inch thick, but it sustained its own weight in a length that would have snapped steel cable like string and it held up, besides, an oval, nearly globular object that was five feet in diameter and had windows and hatches underneath.

The ovoid shape came through the last layer of cloud-stuff in deep darkness. The clouds were higher than the mountains above Seco Valley, just then, but they cut off all sight of the moon or stars. The thing from the sky descended, and seemed to see the jagged mountain-tops. It may have had some sort of drive in it, permitting it to maneuver at the end of its string. It sheered away from the mountains and went down and down—bobbing a little as if the thread were slightly elastic—until it was a bare five hundred feet above the valley floor. There it paused, and presently dropped another hundred feet, and then a hundred and fifty, and then quite slowly until it hung wavering in the darkness not more than forty feet or so above the valley-bottom. There it became still, as if thinking deeply or preparing for something important.

Nobody saw it. The only human dwelling within thirty miles was Brady's shack, and he was over in San Felice waiting for Steve. Nobody heard it. Not even lizards or rattlesnakes or such. There weren't any. There had been rain here two days ago, but no trace of moisture remained. There was nothing living in the valley.

There came a small noise in the air. It was a faint, wavering, far-away muttering that gradually increased in volume. It rose to a droning hum, and the hum became a growl and the growl became a roar. Then the Chicago-to-Los-Angeles plane roared into view above the mountains to the east. It was well above the peaks, but barely below the ceiling of cloud. It was invisible, of course—merely a high-up bellowing of motors and two winking wing-tip lights of red and green which swam toward the zenith while the thing from the sky hung motionless above the desolation of Seco Valley.

Up aloft, apparently something happened. There was a momentary check, perhaps, in the sound of one of the four motors. But the plane did not check or swerve. A propeller hitting an impossible cord in mid-air and cutting through it with a whirling blade, might make such a momentary pause. But the plane drove on.

The thing from the sky, though, jerked violently upward. It lunged, and went careening off to one side, and then fell like a plummet to the floor of the valley. It crashed. Something crackled. There was a sound like an explosion, only wrong. It wasn't air expanding from high pressure, but air expanding into a near-vacuum. Then there was silence, and then a hurried, pattering noise as thousands upon thousands of feet of quarter-inch line came leaping down out of the night sky. It coiled over the smashed ovoid. It went wavering in huge loops and tanglings over a space a hundred feet across.

The plane's navigation-lights swam across the sky. They went beyond the western mountain-tops and vanished. The sound of motors went down from a bellow to a growl, to a drone, to a hum, and then to a faint, faint muttering. Then it could not be heard any longer. There was silence in Seco Valley for a long time.

Ultimately, though, something crawled painfully out of the smashed oval shape, and went helplessly around its outside. It tugged hopelesly at this and that. Then it waited, watching the sky. Nothing happened, though it waited by its shattered vehicle until almost daylight—until false dawn showed it the mountains all about.

But when dawn came there was merely a cryptic mass of plastic wreckage, and thousands of feet of plastic cord—and nothing else. And nothing living was to be seen in Seco Valley.

That was Saturday. Sunday morning Steve Hansun arrived, with Brady and two burros and Brady's dog Gyp. They got to the edge of the valley while life in it was still conceivable—within an hour or two of sunrise. By eight o'clock the valley was warm, and by nine it was hot, and by ten it was like an oven heated by carbon arcs. After that it really got torrid. It wouldn't have been a joke to fry an egg on a sunbaked stone at midday. It would have been a practical method of cookery if any man could imagine eating in such heat. There were mirages, and the rocky hillsides beyond the valley danced insane sarabands from the heat, and the fact that rain had fallen here seemed merely an historical oddity. It had nothing to do with present fact.

Steve Hansun hoped differently. Botanists still find it amazing that plants can live as bone-dry seeds in Death Valley for ten years, and then sprout and blossom and fruit and go to seed again after just one of the decennial rainstorms. Seco Valley was drier still. If Steve could find plants which had survived thirty years of absolute aridity; if he could find plants springing up in Seco Valley after a rain, he would have made an important scientific discovery and could write a paper about it for a scientific publication which nobody would ever read. That was why he'd come.

He saw the wreckage out near the middle of the valley. The two burros, then, were picking their way down a rocky trail that probably had never been used two dozen times since time began. Steve stared, and saw sunlight reflected from something polished, and a whitish indefinite something all around. He couldn't make out what he saw.

"What's that yonder?" he asked. "Could it be a crashed plane?"

Brady squinted, and said nothing.

"We'll take a look," said Steve. "There might be somebody still alive in it."

Brady didn't reply in words. The burros followed patiently to the valley floor. Gyp, the dog, sniffed at a sunbaked rock. But he'd been in desert country before. He restrained himself. The two men and the burros and the dog struck out across Seco Valley toward the wreckage.

The ground was uneven. They came upon wind-eroded boulders which barred their way. The had to back-trail and go around them. They came to dunes of powdery stuff and their feet sank into them as if into volcanic ash. By nine—when it was first really hot—they were only well started out from the valley's edge. By ten they were only part-way to the wreckage. The burros looked irritatingly resigned. Gyp panted heavily and his tail already drooped. By eleven, the dog was utterly dispirited. He trailed the burros in bitter misery, loping gingerly across scorching sand to find a bit of shadow where he could stand without singeing his paws, and then looking miserably for another place to which he could make another dash. The sun was a ball of intolerable fire. Exposed flesh stung when in full sunlight. Steve said:

"Nobody could live long in that plane."

Brady said:

" 'Ain't a plane. I saw it clear a while back."

Steve didn't ask what it could be. It was too hot to talk. As a botanist, he kept his eyes open for signs of vegetation. In Death Valley, the improbable dryland-plants appear as green threads on the third or fourth day after the once-a-decade rainfall. The rain here had been not quite three days since. Nothing showed, yet. But Steve watched carefully as he walked.

Everything was barren. Everything was desiccated past belief. The only sign of the rainfall was that in two or three places sheltered from the sun the ground still showed the pittings of raindrops. Once, too, Steve dug at a hollow place between two hillocks. A foot down he came to very, very faintly dampish soil. He continued to dig, and a foot further down came upon dryness again. There was a thin, underground layer of moisture from the rain. Nothing more.

He got up without words and followed after Brady. He noticed Gyp, his tail drooping, suffering miserably from the scorching sand beneath his paws.

It was half-past twelve when Brady came to a halt beside the thing they had headed for. He grunted expressively. Steve stared. It wasn't the plane he'd guessed at. He didn't know what it was. He saw some thousands of feet of thin, quarter-inch line. It wasn't woven of small fibres. It was one fibre. He saw a smashed object he couldn't reconstruct in his mind, because he wasn't prepared to imagine a plastic globe of five-foot diameter smashed flat in Seco Valley. He did see some piles of spilled or dumped stuff that looked like ashes. Only he thought absurdly of seeds.

First, of course, he tried to find out if anything human remained in the wreckage. He found nothing except some plastic items which were rather like machinery—except that machinery isn't made of plastic—and were part of the smashed globe. Gyp hunted for shade, and then suddenly began to growl. His growlings changed to snarling barks. He was suffering from the heat, but this was even more compelling. He faced an opening in the cryptic thing of plastic and snarled and growled and barked all at once, working himself almost up to hysterics. Steve bent over to look into the hole. It wasn't a big opening. Something could have gotten out through it, but nothing remained inside. As he bent over, staring, he caught a faint whiff of an absolutely indescribable odor. It wasn't pleasant or unpleasant. It was simply unparalleled. He'd never smelled anything even remotely like it.

"Brady!" he said, puzzled. "What's this smell?"

Brady came. He smelled. He spat and grunted.

Gyp backed away from the hole in the plastic, his hackles raised, snarling and barking and growling furiously. He found a trail. He trotted along it, making infuriated noises. He stopped and looked at his master. He forgot even his scorching feet. He made noises of unseemly indignation and rage.

"Now—what the hell?" said Steve.

Brady regarded his dog, frowning.

"Something he never smelled before," he said curtly. "Nor me either. That's the trail, though. Follow it?"

"It doesn't make sense!" protested Steve. "What's this thing, anyhow? And these things that look like seeds. . . ."

He picked up a handful from a pile. There was a tiny hard core to each one. There was a fluffy substance about the core, rather like a strand of cobweb made frizzy and wrapped loosely around something. They were seeds. Wind would carry them anywhere. Steve frowned in concentration. He looked at the small, shining piles. Then he blinked and bent down.

The seeds at the very edges of the pile looked different, somehow. He picked up a few, with sand. From each seed a filament as thin as the thinnest cobweb penetrated the sand. Gossamer seemed to trail from Steve's fingers. He knelt and dug carefully.

A foot and a half down he came to the ever-so-faintly-moistened layer which was the result of the first rain in Seco Valley for thirty years. He found something else there, too. Each thread of gossamer enlarged in the dampish soil into a root. The separate rootlets looked like worms the color of beef-fat. And Steve knew what they were, but it took him time to believe it. Presently he said painfully:

"Brady, those things are seeds! They put a feeler down into the moisture, and they've started to grow. But there simply aren't any plants like those!"

Brady jerked his thumb at the line which was not woven or twisted, but was one single strand of a single substance.

"Ain't any rope like that, either," he observed. Then he looked at Gyp. "Nor any smell like he wants to trail.—Try it?"

Steve hesitated. He tucked a handful of the nacreous small seeds into an envelope and put it in his pocket. He examined the other piles. All were alike. He filled wide-mouthed glass specimen-containers with the seeds and capped them. He put them back in the burro-packs.

"We might as well," he said uneasily. "It looks like there was something alive in there, and it came out and has gone off. It doesn't seem like it could have been a man, though. It might have been a child—but that's not right, either!"

It didn't make sense. Not any of it. Brady poured out water from the supply a burro carried. He offered it to Gyp. The dog drank with feverish thirst. Then he licked Brady's hand and went back to the trail. Again he barked and snarled and growled at it.

The two men followed him toward the hills.

Brady frowned as Gyp went on over the desert, using bad language all the way. Gyp did not usually make such a racket on a trail. The scent was evidently one which agitated him unreasonably. Presently he led the men to a sheltered spot where there was shade. The surface of the ground was slightly crusted from the vanished rain, and there were tracks. More—something had rested on the sand.

Gyp barked and snarled until he seemed to scream hatred at the place where something had apparently lain down. Steve looked. Brady scowled.

"Just what," asked Steve, "would you say made that, Brady?"

"There ain't anything that makes that kinda trail, or that kinda print when it lays down," said Brady curtly. "I'd admire to see that thing. —It ain't big," he added. "A .45 bullet would stop it, sure. I'd like to look it over."

"No bird or animal or lizard," said Steve, as if arguing

with himself. "It came from that—wreckage out in the valley. Hm. . . . We'll track this down, Brady but—we don't shoot too quick."

Brady grunted. They went on. At four in the afternoon Gyp was a badly whipped dog. He was beaten by the heat and the awful dryness. Steve had drunk two canteens of water, despite rigorous self-denial. But Brady had known what to expect. Each of their burros carried water as a full half of its burden. They could go a week and longer without coming upon a water-hole. But they were a silent, dogged crew, the two men and two burros and the dog as they trudged across a waste of incandescent heat and sunshine, with a cloud of fine dry dust rising behind them.

They reached the far side of Seco Valley just at sunset. Glorious colorings filled the sky. Without a word, they began the ascent of the hills. Gyp could barely drag one paw before the other. Brady halted and gave him water. The dog drank as if he would never stop. Then he went back to the trail, growling again.

"Never seen him like this before," said Brady uncomfortably. "He hates whatever he's trailin'. He don't feel like that about mountain lions or anything else. What is it, anyways?"

Steve had been thinking. He'd hunted conscientiously enough for signs of vegetation coming from the rain of Wednesday. But he'd been thinking hard. Seeds which lay on absolutely dry sand and put out threads as fine as gossamer, which wormed their way through a foot and a half of dry soil to find dampness, and there swelled monstrously to greasy-looking rootlets. There wasn't any plant like that. There were no such seeds! And the smashed thing in the valley. It was artificial, certainly. But nobody would make anything like that. The rope—nobody could make anything like that. The scent of the interior of the smashed thing— vaguely, Steve was beginning to imagine it reconstructed into a globe—was so alien that there was no word for it. And Gyp—

"I've got a hunch," said Steve abruptly. "Stop at a level place, Brady. I'm going to put one of those seeds in water. I've got an idea it will surprise us. But the idea of how is crazy! But—anyhow, did you notice how that wreckage was braced?"

Brady grunted negatively.

"It was braced against outside pressure," said Steve. "Like a submarine. The pressure-cabin of the plane I was in was

133

braced against inside pressure pushing out. This was braced against outside pressure pushing in. Mean anything?"

Brady shook his head. They were now perhaps two hundred feet above the valley floor. Brady halted. Steve went to one of the burrows and got out a specimen-jar. He slushed it half full of water—and drank deeply of the rest. He reached in his pocket for the envelope of seeds he had brought. He tried to pull the envelope out. He had trouble. When it came, it ripped to shreds.

A tress of cobwebby threads stretched tenaciously back to his pocket. It was elastic. It was strong. Each thread was infinitesimal, but their total strength was great. As he tugged at them he felt crawling sensations next to his skin. He gasped suddenly and tore off his clothes. The gossamer threads went through his shirt, between the weave of the cloth. Inside there were fat, worm-like objects which began in the fine, silky threads but were themselves swollen and like beef-fat in appearance. They were rootlets, each one developed from a thread from a seed. Each seed in the envelope in Steve's pocket had put out a probe which had worked through his garments to the moisture next his skin. Every thread had swollen hugely in that moisture. Some of them were half the size of a lead-pencil.

The sun sank behind the mountains in a glory of rose and gold. Darkness flowed over the valley which was quite the most arid spot on earth. There was a winking glitter of reflected sunlight from polished plastic.

Steve examined his skin with fresh sweat starting out on him. But it was unbroken. None of the rootlets had made any attempt to secure moisture beyond what the unholy heat of the valley had made available as sweat.

Then Steve shivered, warm as it was from the subheated rocks about him. Without explanation he strapped his removed garments into a bundle and put on others from the pack. His face was pale.

"What now?" asked Brady laconically. "That trail's still good, but Gyp's pretty tired."

"I think we'd better go on," Steve told him. "I want to see whoever or whatever would travel around with seeds like that!"

Gyp lay down, panting, but when the men were ready to move on he got to his feet again. First, though, Steve dropped a seed from the sealed-up container into the half-filled jar of water. He capped it, and they climbed.

Gyp led the way unfalteringly, making angry small noises to himself. Night fell, and for a time it seemed that they

134

might have to stop. But then the moon rose. Gyp went on, spurred by rage. It was notable that the trail they followed did not climb up precipitous places. It went only where not only the men but the burros could follow easily. They climbed two thousand feet above the valley floor. Brady observed, there:

"Never knew a wild critter to hunt so hard for easy climbin'."

"I doubt," said Steve, "that you'd call this creature wild."

"Tame, then?" grunted Brady skeptically.

"Not as far as we're concerned," said Steve.

"What in hell is it?" growled Brady.

"If I told you my guess," said Steve, with care, "you'd knock me cold and sit on my head until you could tie me up to take me to a doctor. Let's look at the bottle I dropped the seed in."

They halted. Steve got out the jar with the water in it. He struck a match. But there was no longer any water in it. The jar was filled with a ropy mass, coiled and curled and twisted into strained convolutions within the confines of the glass container. All the water had vanished. There was only a greasy-seeming root that looked like suet.

—Then a rock stirred overhead. It came bounding down the hillside. Other rocks joined it. A minor landslide began. It grew to a major one. Brady lashed one of the burros swiftly to the shelter of a shaft of stone. Steve followed instantly. The landslide roared by, its edges fifty feet from their place of security. Gyp screamed and howled his hate at the heights above them. The rock-slide reached a cliff-edge and poured off it into space. There were far-away crashings. Then, gradually, the sound ended. For a space there were only individual stones bounding and dancing after the others. Then silence.

Brady said, rumbling:

"Rockslides don't often start at night. Mostly it's daytime, when rocks get het up an' slide."

"Something besides heat started that one," said Steve. "There'll be a break in the trail, I'm guessing. I think we'd better camp. And I think we'd better put Gyp on a leash."

It was all crazy, of course, but Brady turned aside. Here was as good a place as any for a dry camp. He began to unload the burros.

"Nothin' to make a fire with," he grunted.

"No fire," said Steve. "No light. Nothing. And we tie up Gyp, and if he starts to raise Cain we get up fast."

"You got something in your head," said Brady. "What?"

"Bats," said Steve. "Craziness. Insanity. Where'd plants

135

come from that were so crazy for water they'd start as a bone-dry seed and go down a foot and a half to where it was moist? It'd take some evolution to produce a dryland plant like that! Who ever heard of a seed in a man's pocket boring through his clothes to sweat during an afternoon's walk? These seeds work fast! They were developed where it's really dry and water has to be grabbed quick! Where'd you say it was?"

Brady rumbled. He got out their blankets.

"What was that wrecked thing?" he demanded.

"Call it a gizmo or a blurp or a dohinkus," said Steve. "One name's as near as another. I doubt there's any name we'd know, for it. What's your guess?"

"It hung down from that rope," said Brady, with an odd air of stubbornness. "It could ha' been somethin' danglin' from an airship. But why?"

"I'd hate to say what I think," Steve told him.

"Would it've been plantin' seeds?" asked Brady sardonically.

Nothing could be more unlikely or more unreasonable than to plant seeds in Seco Valley. But Steve jumped.

"That," he said, troubled, "that's an idea. It may be true. If it is, it's bad!"

Brady tied up Gyp. Steve lay down in his blankets. His body was exhausted, but his mind would not rest. The only possible explanation was too preposterous. He lay wide-eyed, staring at the stars while all the weariness of the day pounded at his body. Gyp slept. Brady lay still. The burros dozed patiently.

Steve didn't know when he went to sleep, but he was wakened by a crash which sounded like an impact, and then the hysterical screaming and barking of Gyp, who flung himself around frantically at the end of his tether, trying to get loose to go after something up above. Brady was fumbling around.

"Mmmmmh!" he grunted. "Somethin' dropped a rock. Missed."

Another stone fell. And another. They were close.

"Me an' Gyp go up an' settle with that fella—"

"No!" said Steve, swallowing. "There's an overhang here. We move back under it. That's all. Just shift camp. I—I've got an idea. If we—caught up to our friend we might have to kill him, in the dark."   ·

"He's tryin' to kill us!" growled Brady.

"I think," said Steve unsteadily, "that a revolver-shot would scare him away. Just the noise. Try it."

There was a pause. Brady frowned heavily in the darkness. Then his gun bellowed. A .45 shot is incredibly loud in the silence of the mountains. Echoes rang. But it seemed to Steve that he heard a shrill high note that might have been a scream, save that it was so shrill that it was up at the very limit of audibility. Then Gyp went into a fresh frenzy, more terrible than before.

"He'll have run away," said Steve, as if unhappy. "I would, in his place. I—know more than I did before. He hasn't a gun or anything like it, or he'd have used them. He didn't expect to need one when he came. —Reasonable, at that. And he knows we're after him." Then Steve said shakenly, "Poor devil!"

"What is it?" demanded Brady, suspicious. "A crazy guy? It'd have to be a crazy midget by the size of the tracks an' the marks where he laid down!"

Steve said slowly:

"Look, Brady! I—I made a guess down by that wreckage. By all the rules of common sense it was sheer lunacy. Everything that's happened so far fits into it, but it's still crazy. When I see that poor devil I'll tell you what I guessed, and you can laugh at me. But you'd be sure I was out of my head if I told you now."

There was a small noise in the air. It was a faint, wavering, far-away mutter that increased in volume. It became a hum, and then a growl, and then a roaring noise. It was high overhead. Steve jerked his head to stare skyward. The Chicago-to-Los-Angeles plane swam across a skyful of stars. It was invisible, but its red and green winglights moved among the other lights that seemed so much akin to them.

It moved with steady deliberation across the constellations. It went across the mountains on the far side of he valley. It went out of sight. Steve drew a deep breath.

"I was on that plane two nights ago," he said slowly. "Just about this time—and it must have been just about here— there was a funny sort of bump and one of the motors checked for an instant. Then the stewardess came through, smiling, to explain that the ship had probably run into some night-flying bird, but everything was all right."

Brady said:

"Huh?"

"If you're right," said Steve," and the rope we saw was holding up the thing that was wrecked—why—the plane ran into the rope and broke it, or a propeller cut it, or something. That caused the wreck. And—that's the answer! It looks like he was planting seeds, or getting ready to. He'd pick a

137

desert place, of course! He wouldn't expect to be seen. He wouldn't want to be! He couldn't imagine a need for weapons. . . . Oh, the poor devil!"

There was only silence in the hills. But Brady said stubbornly:

"Whoever it was, he tried to kill us."

"And I wouldn't kill him for a million," said Steve wryly. "I'm only afraid he'll make us—if I'm right. We trail him in the morning. We can take turns watching tonight, if you like, but I suspect that shot was a pretty bad experience for him. Anyhow he's unarmed and we've got Gyp. —We'll keep Gyp leashed tomorrow. That poor devil is in the worst fix anybody could imagine, and he couldn't conceive of us being willing to be friendly."

Brady growled:

"I'm gettin' an idea too. Okay, I'll play. But I ain't takin' any chances with him. And," he added deliberately, "I ain't spillin' my guess, either."

He lay down in his blankets. Steve sat up for a long time, looking at the stars. There was no alarm. There was no sound but the faint, faint humming of wind among the heights.

At daybreak, Steve examined the root-plant in the jar. It was no longer white. It was an unpleasant, tawny red. He opened the jar. Its interior was dry. Absolutely, utterly dry. Every atom of the water he had poured into it had been absorbed by the plant growing from the gossamer-covered seed. He felt the thing. Most of its weight was certainly water, but it had no feeling of liquid about it. It felt almost powdery-dry. It was solid. When Brady sat up, blinking, Steve was staring at it, his face a study.

"Huh?" said Brady.

"This plant," said Steve. "It's absorbed all the water, and it's as dry and as hard as wood! There's an ethyl cellulose that makes a solid jelly with two per cent of substance and ninety-eight per cent water. That's considered remarkable. But what per cent is this stuff? If you baked this to dryness I doubt you could weigh the ash! This is a dry-land plant that's never been dreamed about before! It used up all the water in the jar. It turned red. Now it's set to bud and flower. It works fast, this thing!"

Then his eyes narrowed. His face went grim.

"I wonder. . . . We've got to catch our fine feathered friend today," he said with a wrench. "There's not much moisture where those other seeds are, but we can't give them time to seed! —If he gives us the slip, I'll keep Gyp and
138

camp by the wreck while you go on to San Felice with some telegrams." Then an idea struck him and he considered soberly: "Hm. . . . There is a chance, at that . . . But let's get going! Fast."

Brady frowned to himself. He was a big man, and he should have been clumsy, but he was wholly efficient. Within minutes they were on the move, eating out of opened cans as they went up the hillside.

"We start trailin' from where those rocks were dumped on us," he said heavily. "We act careful when we get under places where more rocks could be dumped. Huh?"

"That's all," said Steve, absorbed in his thoughts. "If we see him and he shows fight, you fire a shot. Not at him. The noise will do the trick."

Brady said hesitantly:

"Sound don't carry good when you get up real high. He ain't used to loud noises?"

"Not sharp loud ones," agreed Steve. He stared at Brady.

"Whistles carry better'n a yell, high up," added Brady, his forehead wrinkled. Then he said, "Gets cold up on a mountain-peak, too. But you can get a helluva sunburn when the air's so thin you have to boil a egg ten minutes to get it soft-boiled. This fella—uh—he'd be used to that kinda climate?"

"That—and worse," said Steve. He said after a moment, "He'd be used to air as thin as on top of Mount Everest. That's five miles up."

Gyp burst into frenzied barking. They had reached the spot from which rocks had been toppled on them. Brady held Gyp's leash.

"I—uh—I think I got it," he said slowly. "Y'know—uh—watchin' the stars an' all at night, I got kinda interested, once. I bought some books about stars an' planets an' such. Heavy readin', but I made out. Interestin'."

Then he shrugged.

"I guess we' both crazy the same way," he observed. "Now I kinda figure why you say 'poor devil.' He's a long ways from home. —I won't kill him if I can help it."

They went up and up. Again the trail led only up the gentlest grades. There was no place where it climbed a really steep incline. The burros followed placidly. Gyp settled down to straining, bitter pulling at the tether that held him fast. They were three thousand feet above the valley. They were four thousand feet up. A tiny stone clicked on a hillside. Pebbles rattled down a slope. Steve jerked his eyes up.

He saw a tiny shape, a thousand feet higher still. It moved

with pathetic heaviness and desperate resolution. It was not a human shape. Brady followed his eyes. There was silence. Then:

"That's our friend," said Steve without elation. "He knows we're on his trail. And he knows what he tried to do to us. He probably figures that the plane knocked him down on purpose."

"Yeah," said Brady. "It would look that way to him. He come down, danglin'—an' somethin' cut the rope. He'd figure it was intended."

Steve said restlessly:

"I doubt he'll let us talk to him. He tried to wipe us all out, you know. Wipe out all the human race. I—don't think he's managed it. But he'll expect to be killed. If there were only some way—"

Gyp let out a shrieking clamor. Most dogs are near-sighted, but something seemed to tell him that there above him was the creature whose scent he had followed so long. He barked. He growled. He yelped. He screamed his hatred.

The small thing looked down. Probably—very probably—it realized that the men saw it. But it did not hasten. It moved with enormous heaviness, with a terrible weariness, across a talus-covered slope.

"Maybe we can head him off," suggested Steve, watching.

"Safer to trail him," said Brady. "—How'd he try to wipe us all out?"

"Seeds," said Steve, wryly. "Those seeds are dry-land plants. They'd be like weeds, here. We haven't anything that could compete with them for water. They were developed where there isn't any rain. Not even once in centuries. The seeds would be spread by any wind. Started in a wild place—especially a desert like they're accustomed to, only infinitely less rigorous—they'd spread everywhere. Only fifteen per cent of the United States is cultivated, anyhow. They'd get a foothold in our forests and deserts and the open range so we could never wipe them out. They grow too fast. In twelve hours that thing in the bottle is ready to bud. Once they got started, we could never catch up with them."

They went up a steep slope. The small, weary, unhuman object was out of sight. Gyp followed its trail, snarling ferociously. They reached the slope where they'd seen it.

"I keep thinking of him, though," said Steve irrelevantly. "Suppose your weight were suddenly doubled and you were dumped into air so thick and saturated with water that you almost strangled on it. Suppose you had the choice of staying in a place that to you was at least twice as hot as the valley down below, or of climbing mountains—with your weight doubled. Bad, eh? And then suppose you were unarmed, and were being hunted by things you figured would be merciless, and you had no hope of ever seeing another human being again— It would be bad. But that's what the chap up yonder is up against."

"I got that," rumbled Brady. "He's got a tough break. But what harm would weeds do? We got plenty now an' we get along. . . ."

They turned around a projecting column of a cliffside. Gyp yelped. They followed inexorably, two burros and a dog and two men, after the unhuman thing that was weary to death.

"Weeds," said Steve unhappily, "are plants that can survive in a wild state and compete with cultivated plants. You plant vegetables in a field and go away. Weeds will choke them out because the weeds grow faster, seed quicker and more lavishly, and all the rest. Suppose plants like the one I grew in that bottle last night,—suppose they started competing with our plants. They'll thrive in Seco Valley! They'll grow luxuriantly in Death Valley. What'll they do on a fertile hillside or a forest? If they took all the water, and held it, what'd happen to the grass and the bushes and the trees?"

Brady jumped.

"Mmmmmh! Like if prickly pear grew fast, crowdin' out everything else—"

"It's happened where they come from," said Steve sombrely. "Those seeds sprout. They grab moisture and hold it. My guess is that when they've grown as much as they can they flower and seed, so the seeds will be carried by the wind to where they can grab moisture and hold it. If they struck root on Earth and matured quickly enough—and they do—and seeded lavishly enough, which I don't doubt, they could cover our mountains. They could cover our plains. They could soak up all the rainfall that fell on mountains and hold it, so that our rivers would dry up and we'd have no water for irrigation. We'd have no pasture-land. And then those seeds could blow onto our farm-lands. In hours the one seed grew to fill the bottle and it's ready to seed now—if it can. Every inch of cultivated land could have to be weeded twice a day. Presently there wouldn't be as much rain. Maybe—I don't know what they'd do to a lake! Grow in it and turn it solid? Suppose seeds fell in the ocean. Would that turn solid? Plants like this would find all the minerals they needed in seawater. Maybe—well—maybe that's what they did to the place this fellow comes from. Maybe that's why it's dry—all the water's locked up in plants like this. He's used to that kind of environ-

141

ment, though, now. Maybe he and his kind want to turn our surroundings into the kind they can live in. If they figure that way and they're right, all they'd need to do would be to plant seeds! Our world would turn tawny-red instead of green. In a few years there wouldn't be any clouds. There'd be ice-caps at the poles, but no oceans or lakes or rivers. And there wouldn't be any people. This chap and his friends could just move in."

Brady scowled. He stared at Steve, who looked sick instead of frightened. He looked unhappy. He looked utterly uncomfortable. But he did not look alarmed.

"Well?" said Brady pugnaciously.

"The plant I grew in the bottle," said Steve. "It used up all the water. It held it. It got bone-dry to the touch, though it was nearly all water, actually. Then it started to bud. —It works fast. But it hasn't gone on to seed. I don't think it will, of itself. I suspect I can make it—and I suspect I'm going to because it will be good business to have a source of those seeds. But I don't think it will seed of itself. I *think* there's a very trivial item involved that our friend's friends couldn't figure on in advance. We can figure it, and we would, but I don't think they could."

They came out upon an open space where a great, bald, rounded dome projected from the mountain as a buttress to the monster still reaching thousands of feet toward the sky. This was five thousand feet above the valley floor. Beyond the great rounded projection there was a vista of space illimitable. Mountain after mountain and valley after valley. It was magnificent.

But the two men had no eyes for it. They saw only a small, non-human figure in the middle of the huge gray dome. It was very much smaller than a man. It was grotesque by earthly standards and it was pathetic by any standard. It staggered as it moved out from the bulk of the mountain. It was exhausted, and undoubtedly it was feverish and enfeebled by temperatures which to it were incredible. And it was alone as no human being has ever yet been alone. It went staggering out from the mountain-flank upon this buttress, where there was nowhere that it could flee.

"Got 'im now!" said Brady. Gyp screamed and yelped shrilly at the staggering thing.

"Barely able to walk," said Steve soberly. "Poor devil! Brady, let me take your pistol. I can probably stun him with the noise, if I have to. I'll go out to him alone and try to make him understand we want to be friendly."

He stepped out in slow pursuit. He held up his hands in the

142

universal human sign of peace. The thing stopped and stared fully at him, wavering on its feet. It was a bare quarter-mile away. Steve went coaxingly toward it, trying with infinite care to give the impression of peaceful intentions to a creature which had no single mental link with man.

The creature turned and shambled on. Steve halted. He called after it. Then he realized that if it was the creature's voice he had heard after the shot of the night before, that his voice would be low-pitched indeed to its ears. His words would sound to it like low-toned, menacing growlings. It went on. Steve suddenly essayed to run, to head it off from the abyss before it.

But the creature seemed to summon a terrible, an infinitely heart-breaking resolve. It lumbered into a wholly desperate and despairing run. The rocky dome sloped downward. The creature moved faster and faster. . . . The rock slanted down. . . .

Steve stopped short. But the creature could not stop. It stumbled and fell and even then it did not stop. It went on, sliding, twisting, turning. . . .

It went out of sight. But it would fall fifteen hundred to two thousand feet before it hit.

Steve went desolately back to Brady.

"You saw what happened," he said tiredly. "Maybe I was stupid. But I didn't know what else to do. If we could have communicated with him, we could have made friends. Maybe we could have communicated with the ship he came from. Maybe— But what's the use?"

"No use," said Brady. His forehead was creased. "But that weed business. . . . You think those red plants are goin' to take over as weeds, like you said?"

Steve went to the burro-pack and looked at the glass jar. He'd left the top off. The coiled, twisted, tawny-red object was exactly as he'd left it. He examined it with vast care.

"No," he said drily. "After all—not a chance. These buds haven't developed and now they won't, because these plants work fast. It went so far and no farther. —The limit of a plant's normal northward range and the time of year it blooms is determined by the amount of sunshine it needs each day before it can form a flower and seeds afterward. Spring plants don't need much. Midsummer plants need more. The critical factor is ultraviolet. We've got a thick atmosphere, here on earth. Not much ultraviolet gets through, by comparison with what arrives from the sun. But this plant developed where the air was so thin that the ultraviolet was ten or twenty times stronger than on Earth. So this plant will

143

never bloom or make seed on Earth unless we put it under a battery of ultraviolet lights. Which we will. We'll want more seeds than I've got.'"

Then Steve said in rueful satisfaction:

"But will they be swell arid-area plants! We may have to tinker with them with X-rays to get them to mutate, and we may have to propagate favorable varieties by slips, but with a plant that'll grow where these do, we'll wind up with cattle-food and maybe an industrial raw material and—and—"

Brady said:

"We'd oughta try to find that fella's body."

"Naturally," said Steve. "I wish we could have made friends. . . ."

But there simply hadn't been any way to do it. On the way down to the foot of the mountain-buttress, Steve found himself thinking more and more regretfully about that failure. There were other matters to be attended to, of course. The wreckage had to be retrieved and investigated. That should be a government job. There might be some very useful stuff.

(There was. It's not yet publicly admitted, but four new plastics, a prime-mover principle, and something that looks like the germ of a space-drive are still top secret products of the investigation. Even the dry-area plants—there are four varieties, so far, with possibilities that look too good to be true—are not yet released. And of course the proof that intelligent life exists on other planets and that space-travel is attainable can't be officially acknowledged because it would create panic if revealed before we have adequate space-ships of our own.)

But that morning, and that day on the way out to the wreckage in Seco Valley, and the following two days on the way to San Felice to pass on what he'd found to the proper quarters—during that time Steve didn't think of the affair in technological terms. He was haunted by the end of his and Brady's hunt for the body of the creature who had plunged to his death rather than be captured by men who wished to be his friends. It was tragic that all their efforts were in vain. They found where the body fell, but they couldn't climb a vertical, seamless cliff to reach the shelf on which the poor devil of a Martian had fallen—alone of his kind on an alien planet—and to which the buzzards were already hurrying.

THE END

144

www.ingramcontent.com/pod-product-compliance
Lightning Source LLC
Chambersburg PA
CBHW020140180626
46810CB00004B/1647